Praise for
KRISTINE KATHRYN RUSCH

Kristine Kathryn Rusch's crime stories are exceptional,
both in plot and in style.

—Ed Gorman
Mystery Scene Magazine

Rusch is a great storyteller.

—*RT Book Reviews*

Kristine Kathryn Rusch is one of the best writers in
the field.

—*SFRevu*

[Retrieval Artist Miles Flint is] one of the top ten
greatest science fiction detectives of all time.

—*io9*

The SF thriller is alive and well, and today's leading
practitioner is Kristine Kathryn Rusch.

—*Analog*

A well-conceived, well-executed novel.
—*The New York Times Book Review*
on *Alien Influences*

Also by
Kristine Kathryn Rusch

Alien Influences
Snipers

The Retrieval Artist Series:

The Retrieval Artist (A Short Novel)
The Disappeared
Extremes
Consequences
Buried Deep
Paloma
Recovery Man
The Recovery Man's Bargain (A Short Novel)
Duplicate Effort
The Possession of Paavo Deshin (A Short Novel)
Anniversary Day
Blowback

The END of the WORLD

KRISTINE KATHRYN RUSCH

*wmg*PUBLISHING

The End of the World

Published 2013 by WMG Publishing
www.wmgpublishing.com
First published in *Alien Crimes*, edited by Mike Resnick, The
Science Fiction Book Club, 2007
Cover art copyright © Rolffimages/Dreamstime
Book and cover design copyright © 2013 by WMG Publishing
Cover design by Allyson Longueira/WMG Publishing
ISBN-13: 978-0-615-76463-4
ISBN-10: 0-615-76463-0

The END of the WORLD

THEN

THE AIR REEKED OF SMOKE.

The people ran, and the others chased them.

She kept tripping. Momma pulled her forward, but Momma's hand was slippery. Her hand slid out, and she fell, sprawling on the wooden sidewalk.

Momma reached for her, but the crowd swept Momma forward.

All she saw was Momma's face, panicked, her hands, grasping, and then Momma was gone.

Everyone ran around her, over her, on her. She put her hands over her head and cringed, curling herself into a little ball.

She made herself change color. Brown-gray like the sidewalk, with black lines running up and down.

Dress hems skimmed over her. Boots brushed her. Heels pinched the skin on her arms.

No spikes, Momma always said. *No spikes or they'll know.*

So she held her breath, hoping the spikes wouldn't break through her skin because she was so scared, and her side hurt where someone's boot hit it, and the wooden sidewalk bounced as more and more people ran past her.

Finally, she started squinching, like Daddy taught her before he left.

Slide, he said. *A little bit at a time. Slide. Squinch onto whatever surface you're on and cling.*

It was hard to squinch without spikes, but she did, her head tucked in her belly, her hair trailing to one side. More boots stomped on it, pulling it, but she bit her lower lip so that she wouldn't have to think about the pain.

She was almost to the bank door when the sidewalk stopped shaking. No one ran by her. She was alone.

She flattened herself against the brick and shuddered. Her skin smelled of chewing tobacco, spit and beer from the saloon next door.

She had shut down her ears, but she finally rotated them outward. Men were shouting, women yelling. There was pounding and screaming and a high-pitched noise she didn't like.

If they found her flattened against the brick, they'd know. If they saw the spikes rise from her body, they'd know. If they saw her squinching, they'd know.

But she couldn't move.

She was shivering, and she didn't know what to do.

NOW

THE CALL DIDN'T COME THROUGH CHANNELS. It rang to Becca Keller's personal cell.

Chase Waterston hadn't even said hello.

"Got a problem at the End of the World," he'd said, his usually self-assured voice shaky. "Can you get here right away? Just you."

Normally, she would have told him to call the precinct or 911, but something stopped her. Probably that scared edge to his voice, a sound she'd never heard in all the years she'd known him.

She drove from the center of downtown Hope to the End of the World, a drive that, in the old days, would have taken five minutes. Now it took twenty, and the only thing that kept her from being annoyed at the traffic were the mountains, bleak and cold, rising up like goddesses at the edge of Hope.

Hope was a mountain city, but its terrain was high desert. Vast expanses of brown still marked the outskirts of town, although the interior had lost much of its desert

3

feel. By the time she passed the latest ticky-tacky development, she hit the rolling dunes of her childhood. Even though she had on the air-conditioning, the smell of sagebrush blew in—full of promise.

If she kept going straight too much farther, she'd hit small windy roads filled with switchbacks that led to now-trendy ski resorts. If she turned right, she'd follow the old stage coach route over the edge of the mountains into the Willamette Valley where most of Oregon's population lived.

The End of the World was an ancient resort at the fork between the mountain roads and the old stagecoach route. At the turn of the previous century, some enterprising entrepreneur figured travelers who were taking the narrow road toward the Willamette Valley would welcome a place to rest and recover from the long dusty trip.

Now bumper-to-bumper traffic filled that wagon route, which had expanded to a four-lane highway. Hope actually had a real rush hour, thanks to ex-patriate Californians, retired baby boomers, and ridiculously cheap housing.

Chase was rebuilding the resort for those baby boomers and Californians. For some reason, he thought they'd want to stay in a hundred-year-old hotel, with a view of the mountains and the river, even in the heat of the summer and the deep cold of the desert winter.

Becca steered the squad with her left hand and fiddled with the air-conditioner with her right, wishing her own car was out of the shop. No matter what she did, she couldn't get the squad car cooled. Nothing seemed to be working properly. Or maybe that was the effect of the heat.

It was a hundred and three degrees, and the third week without rain. The radio's most recent weather report promised the temperature would reach one hundred and eight by the time the day was over.

Finally, she reached the construction site.

Chase had set up the site so that it only blocked part of the ever-present wind and as a consequence, the dust billowed across the highway with the gusts.

The city had cited Chase twice for the hazard, and he'd promised to fix it just after the Fourth of July holiday. It looked like he'd been keeping his word, too. A huge plastic construction fence leaned against the old building. Graders and post-diggers were parked on the side of the road.

Nothing moved. Not the cats Chase had been using to dig out the old parking lot, not the crane he'd rented the week before, and not the crew, most of whom sat on the backs of pick-up trucks, their faces blackened with dust and grime and too much sun. She could see their eyes, white against the darkness of their skins, watching her as she turned onto the dirt path that Chase had been using as an access road.

He was waiting for her in the doorway of what had once been a natatorium. Built over an old underground spring, the Natatorium had once boasted the largest swimming pool in Eastern Oregon. There was some kind of pipe system which pumped water into the pool, keeping it perpetually cold. In the Natatorium's heyday, the water had been replaced daily.

Behind the Natatorium was the old five-story brick hotel that still had the original fixtures. No vandals had ever attacked the place. Even the windows were intact.

Becca had gone inside more than once, first as an impressionable twelve-year-old, and ever since, part of her believed the rumors that the hotel was haunted.

She pulled up beside the Natatorium door, in a tiny patch of shade provided by the overhanging roof. She got out and the blast-furnace heat hit her, prickling sweat on her skin almost instantly. Apparently the air conditioner had been working in the piece-of-crap squad after all.

Chase watched her. His lips were chapped, his skin fried blackish red from the sun. He had weather-wrinkles around his eyes and narrow mouth. His hair was cropped short, and over it he wore a regulation hardhat. He clutched another one in his left hand, slapping it rhythmically against his thigh.

"Thanks for coming, Becca," he said, and he still sounded shaken.

The tone was unfamiliar, but the expression on his face wasn't. She'd seen it only once, after she'd told him she wanted out, that his values and hers were so different, she couldn't stomach a relationship any longer.

"What do you got, Chase?" she asked.

"Come with me." He handed her the hardhat he'd been holding.

She took it as a gust of wind caught her short hair and blew its clipped edges into her face. She slipped the hardhat on, and tucked her hair underneath it, then followed Chase inside the building.

It was hotter inside the Natatorium, and the air smelled of rot and mold. She usually thought of those as humidity smells, but the Natatorium's interior was so dry that it was crumbly.

The floor was shredded with age, the wood so brittle that she wondered if it would hold her weight. Most of the walls were gone, the remains of them piled in a corner. Chase had gutted the interior.

When she had been a girl, she had played in this place. Her parents had forbidden her to come, which made it all the more inviting. The rot and mold smells had been present even then. But the walls had still been up, and there had been some ancient furniture in here as well, made unusable by weather and critters chewing the interior.

She used to stand inside the entrance with the door open, the stream of sunlight carrying a spinning tunnel of dust motes. When she closed her eyes halfway, she could just imagine the people arriving here after a long day of travel, happy to be in a place of such elegance, such warmth.

But now even that sense of a long ago but lively past was gone, and all that remained was the shell of the building itself—a hazard, an eyesore, something to be torn down and replaced.

Chase's boots echoed on the wood floor. He led her along the edges, pointing at holes closer to the center. She wondered if any of his employees had caused the holes, walking imprudently across the floor, foot catching on the weak spot, and then slipping through.

He was taking her to the employees' staircase in the back. When they reached it, she saw why. It was made of metal. Rusted metal, but metal all the same. Someone had recently bolted the stairs into the wall, probably under Chase's orders. A metal hand railing had been reinforced as well.

Chase looked over his shoulder to make sure she was following. She caught a glimpse of something in his face—reluctance? Fear? She couldn't quite tell—and then, as suddenly as it appeared, it was gone.

He went down the steps two at a time. She followed. Even though the handrail had been rebolted, the metal still flaked under her hand. The bolts might hold if she suddenly fell through the stairs but she wasn't sure if the railing would.

The smell grew stronger here, as if the mold had somehow managed to survive the dry summers. The farther down she went, the cooler the air got. It was still hot, but no longer oppressive.

Chase stopped at the bottom of the stairs. He watched her come down the last few, his gaze holding hers. The intensity of his gaze startled her. It was vulnerable, in a way she hadn't seen since their first year together.

Then he stepped away so that she could stand on the floor below.

The smell was so strong that it overwhelmed her. Beneath the mold and rot, there was something else, something familiar, something foul. It made the hair rise on the back of her neck.

"That way," Chase said, and this time she wasn't mistaking it. His voice was shaking. "I'll wait here."

She frowned at him, and then kept going. The floor here was covered in ceramic tile, chipped and broken, but sturdy. She wondered what was beneath it. Ground? Old-fashioned concrete? Wood? She couldn't tell. But the floor didn't creak here, and it felt solid.

A long wall hid everything from view. A door stood open, sending in sunlight filled with dust motes, just like she remembered. Only there shouldn't be sunlight here. This was the basement, the miraculous swimming pool, the place that had helped make the End of the World famous.

She stepped through the door.

The light came from the back wall—or what had been the back. Chase's crew had destroyed this part of the building.

The basement of the End of the World was open to the air for the first time since it had been completed.

That strange feeling she'd had since she reached the bottom of the stairs grew. If the basement wasn't sealed, then the stench shouldn't have been so strong. The old air should have escaped, letting the freshness of the desert inside.

Some of the heat had trickled in, but not enough to dissipate the natural coolness. She stepped forward. The tile on the other side of the pool was hidden under mounds of dirt. The pool itself was half destroyed, but the cat which had done the damage wasn't anywhere near it. She could see the big tire tracks, scored deeply into the sandy earth, as if the cat itself had been stuck or if the operator had tried to escape in a hurry.

They had uncovered something. That much was clear. And she was beginning to get an idea as to what it was.

A body.

Given the smell, it had to have died here recently. Bodies didn't decay in the desert—not in the dry air and the sand. Inside a building like this, there might be standard decomposition, but considering how hot it had been, even that seemed unlikely.

She'd have to assume cause of death was suspicious because the body had been located here. And then she'd have to figure out a way to find out whose body it was.

She was already planning how she'd conduct her case when she stepped off the tile onto a mound of dirt, and peered into the gaping hole, and saw—

Bones. Piles of bones. Recognizable bones. Femurs, hip bones, pelvic bones, rib cages. Hundreds of human bones. And more skulls than she could count.

She rocked back on her heels, pressing her free hand to her face, the smell—the illogical and impossible smell— now turning her stomach.

A mass grave, of the kind she'd only seen in film or police academy photos.

A mass grave, anywhere from a hundred to seventy-five years old.

A mass grave, in Hope. She hadn't even heard rumors of it, and she had lived here all her life.

"Son of a bitch," she said.

"Yeah," Chase said from the stairs, "I couldn't agree more."

THEN

THE SCREAMING SENT RIPPLES THROUGH HER. She couldn't complete the change. She couldn't even assume the color and texture of the brick.

Tears pricked her eyes. Tears, as big a giveaway as her hair, her fingers, her ears. Somehow, when she stopped the spikes, she stopped all her abilities.

Or maybe it was just the fear.

A door squeaked open, then boots hit the sidewalk. Polished boots with only a layer of black dust along the edge. Men's boots, not the dainty things Momma tried to wear.

She tried to will the shivering away, but she couldn't.

She couldn't move at all.

Not that she had anywhere to go.

She could only pray that he wouldn't look down, that he wouldn't see her, that she would be safe for just a little longer.

NOW

BECCA STARED AT THE HOLE. She couldn't even count all the skulls, rising like white stones out of the dirt. Not to mention the rib cages off to one side or the tiny bones lying in a corner, bones that probably belonged in a hand or a foot.

She couldn't do much on her own. But she could find out where that stink was coming from.

She turned around and headed for the stairs.

Chase tipped his hardhat back, revealing his dark eyes. "Where're you going?"

"To get some things from my evidence bag," Becca said.

"You're not going to call anyone, are you?" he asked.

She stopped in front of him. "I can't take care of this alone. You should know that."

He leaned against the railing, that assumed casual gesture which meant he was the most distressed. "This'll ruin me, Becca. Half my capital is in this place."

"You told me no good businessman ever invests his own money," she snapped, mostly because she was surprised.

He shrugged. "Guess I'm not a good businessman."

But he was. He had restored three of the downtown's oldest buildings, making them into expensive condominiums with views of the mountains. Single-handedly, he'd revitalized Hope's downtown, by adding trendy stores that the locals claimed would never succeed (yet somehow they did, thanks to the "foreigners," as the Californians were called) and restaurants so upscale that Becca would have to spend half a week's pay just to eat lunch.

"You knew I'd go by the book when you called me here," she said, more sharply than she intended. He'd gotten to her. That was the problem; he always did.

"I thought maybe we could talk. They're old bones. If we can get someone to recover them and keep it quiet—"

"How many workers saw this?" she asked. "Do you think they'll keep it quiet?"

"If I pay them enough," he said. "And if we move the bones to a proper cemetery."

"Is that what you think this is?" she asked. "A graveyard?"

"Isn't it?" He seemed genuinely surprised. "It was so far out in the desert when this place was built that it's possible—no, it's probable—that the memory of the graveyard got lost."

"I saw at least two ribcages with shattered bones, and several skulls looked crushed."

His lips trembled, and it was a moment before he spoke. "The equipment could have done that."

But he didn't sound convinced.

"It could have," she said. "But we need to know."

"Why?" he asked.

She looked over her shoulder. That patch of sunlight still glinted through the hole in the wall. The dust motes still floated. If she didn't look down, the place would seem just as beautiful and interesting as it always had.

"Because someone loved them once. Someone probably wants to know what happened to them."

"Someone?" He snorted. "Becca, the pool was put over a tennis court that was built at the turn of the 20th century. No one remembers these people. Only historians would care."

He paused, and she felt her breath catch.

Then he said, "This is my life."

He used a tone and inflection she used to find particularly mesmerizing. Once she told their couples therapist that with that tone, he could convince her to do anything, and that was when the therapist told her that she had to get out.

"It's a crime scene," Becca said, knowing that the argument was weak.

"You don't know that for sure, and even if it is, it's a hundred years old," he said.

"Then what's the smell?"

He frowned, clearly not understanding her.

"This is a desert, Chase. Bodies buried in dirt in a dry climate don't decay. They mummify."

He blinked. He obviously hadn't thought of that.

"And," she said, "even if they had decayed because of some strange environmental reason particular to this basement, they wouldn't smell after a hundred years."

That guarded expression had returned to his face. Only his eyes moved now.

"Maybe it's something small," he said. "A mouse, someone's lost cat."

She shook her head. "Smell's too strong, and over the entire building. If it were something small, the smell would have faded back when you broke open that wall."

"Not when it was dug up?" he asked, seeming surprised.

"No," she said. "Is that when you first smelled it?"

"That's when they called me."

They, meaning his crew. She frowned at him, wondering if he was going to blame them.

But for what? A smell?

She'd have to find the source before she made assumptions.

And that, she knew, was going to be hard.

THEN

A HAND TOUCHED HER SHOULDER. A human hand, warm and gentle. Another shivery ripple ran through her. She still had a shoulder; she hadn't gotten rid of that either. How silly she must look, plastered against the brick wall like a half formed younglin.

Screams still echoed. The shouts had died down, although sometimes they rose up altogether, like a group got excited about something.

"You're one of them, aren't you?"

Male voice, human, just as gentle as the hand. She couldn't stop shivering.

"I won't hurt you."

She resisted the urge to rotate an eye upwards, so that she could see more than the boot.

"But you better come with me before they find you."

That did startle her. Her eye moved before she could stop it. It formed above her shoulder. He jumped back slightly when her eye appeared, but his hand never left her skin, even though it was finally turning tannish-red like the brick.

She'd seen him before. Daddy had laughed with him in the good days. He had slicked-back hair and a narrow face and kind eyes.

He crouched beside her, and looked right at her eye, like it didn't bother him, even though she knew it did. He wouldn't've jumped like that if it didn't.

"Please," he said, "come with me. I don't know when they're coming back. And someone might see us. Please."

She had to form a mouth. Her nose remained, tucked against her stomach from when she'd formed a ball, but her mouth had disappeared when she had tried to take on the appearance of the wooden sidewalk.

It took all her strength to make the mouth come out near the eye, and from the look of disgust that passed over his face, she still didn't look right. Her hair was on the other side of her body, and her eye was just above her shoulder. The mouth had probably come out on what would have been her back if she put herself together right.

Right being human.

That's what Momma said.

Momma.

"Please," he said again, and this time, she heard panic in his voice.

"Stuck," she said.

"Oh, Christ." He looked up and down the street, then at the buildings across from it.

He seemed younger than she remembered, or maybe she was as bad at telling human ages as Momma was.

"How do we get you unstuck?" he asked.

She didn't know. She'd never been like this, not this scared, not all by herself.

She tried to shrug and felt her other shoulder form into the wood. A splinter dug into her skin, and her entire body turned red with pain.

"What a mess," he said, and she didn't know if he meant her or what was going on or how scared they both seemed to be.

She willed herself to let go, but she was attached to the brick, and she'd lost control of half her body functions. Daddy said fear would do that.

Whatever happens, baby, he'd say, *you have to trust us. You have to believe we'll get together again. Let that be your strength, so that you never, ever succumb to fear.*

But he'd been gone for a long time now. And Momma hadn't come back for her, even though people were screaming.

The man tried to pry a flat corner of her skin from the edge of the brick. She could feel the tug, saw his face scrunch up in disgust when he got to the sticky underneath part.

"How'd you get there?" he asked.

"Squinched," she said.

"Squinched." He didn't understand. And she spoke his language, she knew she did. She formed the right mouth, she'd been using the words for a long time now, and she knew how they felt inside her brain and out.

"Can you show me?" he asked. "Can you squinch onto my arm?"

She wasn't supposed to squinch to a human. Momma was strict about that. Like there was something bad about it, something awful would happen.

But something awful was happening now.

The screams…

"No," she said, even though that had to be a lie. Momma and Daddy wouldn't forbid something if she couldn't've done it in the first place.

"God," he said, then looked down the street where the screams had come from. Where the shouts had grown more and more angry every time they rose up.

Right now, it was quiet, and she hated that more.

She hated it all.

"Stay here," he said.

He stood up, letting go of her shoulder. The warm vanished, and the fear rose even worse. Her other shoulder disappeared, and she felt the spikes, threatening to appear.

She had to close both eyes and will the spikes away.

When she opened the eyes, he was gone.

She moved the eyes all over her skin, looking for him, and she didn't see him at all.

The street was still empty, and too quiet.

Then, faraway, someone laughed. A mean, nasty, brittle laugh.

She folded her ears inside her skin, and willed herself flat, hoping, this time, that it would work.

NOW

BECCA CLIMBED THE STAIRS, clinging to the handrail, the rust flaking against her palms. She had to call for help. At most, she needed a coroner, and probably a few officers just to search for the source of that smell.

But she felt guilty about calling. Chase used to talk about restoring the End of the World when she'd met him. He had brought her out here on their first date, even though she'd told him that she had explored the property repeatedly when she was a child.

Maybe they'd be able to keep this out of the paper, particularly if it turned out to be a graveyard or a dumping ground. But even that probably wouldn't happen.

The newspapers seemed to love this kind of story.

If she reported this, she would condemn Chase's project to a kind of limbo. With so much capital invested, he probably couldn't afford to wait until the legal issues were solved.

She almost turned around to ask him how much time he could give them, but then she'd be compromising the investigation. For all she knew, there was a recently killed human beneath that dirt, and someone (Chase?) was using the old bones to hide it.

Then she shook her head. Not Chase. He was manipulative and difficult, moody and untrustworthy, but he wasn't—nor had he ever been—violent.

She sighed and continued up the stairs. Much as she wanted to help him, she couldn't. She had an obligation to the entire community.

She had an obligation to herself.

The wind hit her the moment she stepped outside. Bits of sand stung her skin, sticking to the sweat. Even with the sun, it now felt cooler out here because of that wind.

The construction workers watched her. She didn't know most of them; the town had grown too big for her to know everyone by sight like she had when she was a child. Many of these workers were Hispanic, some of them probably illegal.

Hispanics expected her to check their papers. She was supposed to do that too, although she never did. She didn't object to people who worked hard and tried to improve their lives.

With one hand, she tipped her hardhat back and nodded toward the workers. Then she opened the squad's driver's door, and winced at the heat which poured out at her. She leaned inside, unwilling to go into that heat voluntarily, and grabbed the radio's handset.

She paused before turning it on, knowing that even that momentary hesitation was a victory for Chase.

Then she clicked the handset and asked the dispatch to send Jillian Mills.

Jillian Mills was the head coroner for Hope and the surrounding counties. She actually worked the job full time, but her assistants were dentists and veterinarians, and one retired doctor.

"You want the crime scene unit?" the dispatch asked. It was standard procedure for a crime scene unit to come with the coroner.

"Not yet," Becca said. "I'm not sure what exactly we have here, except that it's dead."

Which was technically true, if she ignored all the crushed and broken bones.

"Tell her to hurry," Becca added. "It's hot as hell out here and there's a construction crew waiting."

That usually worked to get any city official moving. Lately, the "foreigners" had taken to suing the city if their emergency or official personnel delayed money-making operations, even for a day.

Chase would never do that—he knew that getting along with the city helped his permits go through and his iffy projects get approved—but Becca still used the excuse.

She didn't want to be here any longer than she had to.

She stood, lifted her hardhat, and wiped the sweat off her forehead. Then she closed the door and leaned on it for a moment.

The End of the World.

She wondered if Chase had ever thought that the name might have been prophetic.

THEN

SHE HAD SHUT DOWN HER EARS, and didn't know he had come back until the sidewalk shook. She opened her eyes. He stood above her holding a long wooden box. His mouth was moving, but he kept looking down the street. A single bead of sweat ran down one side of his face.

She unfolded her ears, and said, "What?"

"This can hide you," he said, setting the box on the sidewalk. He glanced at her, then looked away. "Think maybe you can squinch into it?"

He set the box in front of her. It did cover her strangeness from anyone who didn't look too hard.

Her shivering stopped.

"Maybe," she said.

"Well," he said, wiping at that drop of sweat, "the sooner you squinch, the better chance I have of getting you out of here."

That brought a shiver. She looked at the box, saw it had some dirt inside. He had taken it from some kind of storage.

If she just thought about the box—not the screaming (which seemed to be gone? How come it was gone?)—not the way Momma's hand had slipped through hers, not the fall against the sidewalk, not the bruises that still radiated through her skin, maybe then she could squinch to it.

She'd have to stare at it like a younglin, think only of the box, only of the box and becoming part of it…

A long, drawn out scream sent ripples through her.

"Jesus," the man said and closed his eyes.

She squinched. She had to. The scream made her move. She squinched to the edge of the box, then cowered against the back, just a blob, as small as she could make herself.

"Mister?" she said and heard the terror in her voice. She wasn't sure why she was trusting him, but she didn't have a lot of choice.

That scream sounded like Momma.

He looked down, and his shoulders slumped.

"Thank God," he said, and picked up the box.

He tucked it under his arm like it weighed nothing, and hurried back through the door.

NOW

Jillian drove the white coroner's van. Becca's breath caught as she scanned the windshield, looking for an assistant.

There was none. Either none was available, or dispatch conveyed the message about the stalled work crew.

Either way, Becca was grateful.

She finished the last of her water and tossed the bottle in a nearby recycling can. She had waited up here, unwilling to go back inside without Jillian.

Or maybe she had just been unwilling to talk to Chase again.

He had come out of the basement after about ten minutes. He saw her near the squad, shook his head slightly, and sat against one of the cats, his face half-hidden by shade.

She didn't go to talk to him and he didn't talk to her. They both knew the futility of these kinds of arguments. Once again, she and Chase were on opposite paths, and trying to influence each other would only end in misery.

Jillian got out of the van. Her hair was already pulled back and tucked in a net. She was small and delicate, with skin so pale that it almost looked translucent. She seemed fragile at first glance, but Becca had seen her split a corpse's ribcage open with her bare hands.

"What've we got?" Jillian asked.

"I'm not sure," Becca said.

She grabbed the flashlight and gloves from her own kit, as well as the portable radio, and led Jillian inside.

Chase didn't come with them. Instead, he watched them go with the same wariness that his crew had.

Becca was relieved. She half-hoped that Jillian hadn't noticed him, standing in the shade.

They were on the steps to the basement before Jillian said, "This is Chase Waterston's project, isn't it?"

"Unfortunately," Becca said.

Jillian knew Becca's troubles with Chase. It had been no-nonsense Jillian who had listened to Becca's difficulties extricating herself from Chase's world.

I'm a cop, she used to say, it seemed, during every conversation. *I shouldn't be so easily influenced.*

We all have a hook that'll draw us in, Jillian would respond. *He knows how to find yours.*

He did too. There should have been a full team here, along with a crime scene unit.

Jillian probably knew it just from the smell.

She stopped at the bottom of the stairs and looked around. "Where's the body?"

Becca had thought about how to answer that one the entire time she waited for Jillian.

"I don't know where the smell is coming from," Becca said. "But it's not our only problem."

Jillian glanced at her sideways. Becca sighed and led her to the hole.

The sun had moved away from the gap in the wall, no longer sending rays filled with dust motes into the basement. But the light was still strong enough that she didn't need a flashlight to lead Jillian to the dig itself.

"Chase thinks this is an old cemetery," Becca said as she approached.

"You don't," Jillian said, slipping on her gloves. "So you brought me here to be the bad guy."

Maybe she had. Or maybe she just needed someone between her and Chase, someone sensible.

She didn't say any more. Instead, she turned on the flashlight and turned it to the ribcages and skulls.

"Mother of God," Jillian said, touching the tiny cross she wore around her neck even though her Catholicism had lapsed decades ago. "This is going to take an entire team."

"I know," Becca said softly.

They stared for a long moment. Becca didn't move the flashlight beam. Finally, Jillian grabbed it from her and swept the entire large hole. The light caught more bits of bone, scattered throughout the dirt.

"How'd you even get me here?" Jillian asked. "Chase has to know this will ruin him."

"He does." Becca didn't look at Jillian.

"So he called you." Jillian shook her head. "Bastard."

"Jillian, it's bad enough."

"It's bad enough that he thought you'd cover for him."

"He didn't ask that," Becca said. But he had, hadn't he? He asked that this be handled quickly and discreetly and with a minimum of fuss.

Although he stopped arguing when she explained about the smell.

God, she was still making excuses for him, and she was no longer married to him.

"He knows I'm going to do this right."

"He knows," Becca said.

"That'll mean the media'll get wind."

"Let's try to prevent that as long as possible."

"So Chase can save his ass?"

"So that we don't have weirdos contaminating the crime scene."

"You didn't block it off. It could be contaminated now."

Becca pursed her lips. "I kept an eye on everyone."

"I hope so," Jillian said. "I'm going to call for backup."

Becca nodded.

Jillian didn't move, even though she said she was going to. "You think maybe you should take yourself off this investigation?"

Becca'd been thinking about it. "I'm the only qualified investigator we have. Everyone else has been promoted through the ranks and most haven't even completed the crime lab courses."

Because they were only offered in the Willamette Valley, and that was more than two hours from here. The department couldn't afford to lose personnel for days on end just so that they could have classes in criminal justice, classes that the chief—a good ole boy who had worked his way through the ranks without a damn class, thank you—didn't believe anyone needed, not even his detectives.

Jillian sighed. "You've got a conflict."

"No kidding."

"What if Chase is behind the smell?"

Becca almost said, *He isn't*, but she stopped herself in time. "I'll treat him like anyone else."

Even though she knew that was a lie the moment she spoke it.

"No matter what you do, everyone'll think you're soft on him."

"Then everyone'll be supervising me, won't they?" Becca snapped.

Jillian put a hand on her shoulder. "Rethink this, Becca."

Becca sighed. "If this starts leading to Chase, maybe I will."

THEN

HE DIDN'T TAKE HER VERY FAR. She managed to squinch part of herself to the edge of the box, away from his arm, and pop an eye forward.

They were inside the bank. No one else was. The afternoon sun filtered through the large windows, illuminating heavy wooden desks, the wide row of grills that people got money out of or put money into, the safe just behind the far door.

Momma and Daddy had brought her in here early, as part of her training in being "normal" and they explained how banks worked. She used to come with Daddy when he had money to deposit, but Momma didn't know how to get it when he went away.

Momma said maybe he got it, but she had that funny sound in her voice, the one that meant she really didn't believe it. She always sounded sad when she spoke of Daddy, and after a few weeks, she stopped speaking of him at all.

"We can't go far yet," the man said softly. "People'll wonder. They'll probably wonder why I was here, and not with them."

He said that last very very softly. She almost didn't hear him.

He hurried to one of the desks near the back and set the box underneath it with one edge sticking out.

"If you can, stay low," he said. "It's safer."

She wondered how he knew. Maybe he could tell her what was going on. Because she didn't know at all.

Momma had smelled the smoke—they were burning Shantytown, that's what Momma said. Then Momma grabbed her hand and pulled her to the safe place. She didn't know where that was either or what would happen there.

They had run to the middle of the town, right near the fanciest store where Momma liked to look through the windows sometimes, when people caught up to them. Running, just like they were, only the other people's running was different somehow.

Momma seemed really scared now. Some of the men smelled of kerosene, and one of them was laughing even though the edges of his hair were burned off.

Momma pulled and pulled and she was having trouble keeping up and people started looking at them and Momma tried to pick her up but didn't have the strength and she tried to keep running but she couldn't—she was getting so tired—and then she tripped and her hand slipped and she couldn't see Momma and she didn't know where Momma went or why she hadn't come back…

Except for the scream.

She closed her eyes and rolled up into a ball.

She wanted to forget the scream—and she couldn't, no matter how hard she tried.

NOW

JILLIAN STARTED TO WORK in one corner of the hole. Becca took the far end of the basement, using her nose first to see where the smell was the strongest.

Jillian had contacted the crime scene investigators, asking for everyone not just the folks on duty, and another detective as well as some officers to handle the interviews. Becca should have done that. But Jillian was covering for her, getting her off the hook with Chase.

Both of them knew that Chase was their key. He could set up a lot of roadblocks to the investigation, and he might have already done so. Becca would try to find out by remaining close to him, buddying him, if she could.

Jillian wasn't sure that Becca could manipulate him. Hence the request for the second detective.

Becca wasn't going to argue with that. She wasn't going to argue with any of it. Not yet.

But she did know Chase well enough that if he had committed a crime, he wouldn't have done it in a way that would jeopardize his entire fortune. He would have covered it up creatively, hidden the body in the desert or taken it to Waloon Lake or maybe all the way to the ocean.

He was too smart to kill someone and call her. He knew that he could manipulate her, but he also knew that the manipulation didn't always work.

She took a breath. Olfactory nerves grew used to smells, but this one—the smell of rot and decay—never completely vanished. You could live with that smell for weeks, and still recognize it, unlike most other odors. It just wouldn't seem as strong to you as it did to others.

It was still new to her at the moment. And it wasn't coming from this part of the basement.

She walked the perimeter, sniffing the whole way, knowing she would regret this part of the investigation. Strong smells like this remained in the nose and in the memory. She would be able to recall it whenever she wanted.

As if she would want to.

After she finished, she walked the perimeter again, careful to use the same tracks.

Finally, she said, "It's coming from the hole."

"Of course," Jillian said. She had started in one corner as well.

When Becca spoke, Jillian leaned back on her knees, resting on her heels. She brushed her hands together, then surveyed the mess before them.

"This is beyond me," she said. "I don't know how to proceed. We're not trained for a disaster this big. I'm going to have to call in experts."

"Experts?" Becca asked.

"There are people who specialize in dealing with mass graves."

"So this is a graveyard."

Jillian looked at her, as if Becca had deliberately misunderstood her.

"Mass graves. Like the ones they found in Iraq or Bosnia or Nazi Germany."

Becca let out a small breath. The air felt thicker than desert air usually did. The odors seemed to be getting worse, not better.

"That's what this is? Some kind of massacre?"

"I don't know for sure. That's why I want experts. You want to protect Chase—"

Becca started to deny it, but then that was silly. She did want to protect Chase.

"—but I want to protect Hope."

It took her a moment to understand what Jillian had said. "Protect Hope?"

"How much history do you know, Becca?" Jillian asked.

"I know enough to know that no large group of people has ever died in Hope. We still have our Chinatown, and we were one of the havens for blacks, even when the State of Oregon constitutionally banned them. We had that in school, Jillian, remember?"

"You think people talk about massacres?"

"I think people remember," Becca said. "I think massacres don't stay buried forever."

Jillian looked at the dirt before her. A snapped femur was only a few inches from her knees.

"You're right," Jillian said. "Nothing stays buried forever."

THEN

"WHAT'S YOUR NAME?" he asked after a little while.

The question startled her.

The bank had been so quiet, even though she had kept one ear on top and an eye prepared. She could control the ears and the eyes and sometimes the mouth, but she still hadn't got control over anything else. The shivers came less now, but they still came, rippling through her like water.

"It's okay," he said. "We're still alone."

Like that was the problem. Her family tried not to name anything. Names made items rigid.

Still, her parents had given her a human name, just so everyone had something to call her, and Momma said the name made it easier for her to keep her shape.

Maybe if she thought about it now...

He peered under the desk. "Are you all right?"

Another shiver ran through her and she couldn't find her mouth.

"They're not back yet."

If she had her human form, she'd nod. But she didn't. Then the mouth popped forward.

He moved away so fast, he hit his head on the underside of the desk.

"Sorry," he said. "You startled me."

"Sarah," she said.

"Hmm?" He frowned at her.

"I'm Sarah."

"Oh." He bit his upper lip, pulling it inward. "I'd thought maybe something more unusual…."

He stopped talking, wiped a hand over his mouth, then smiled.

"How about a last name?"

A second name. Momma had explained that too. The second name described your clan. The first name was just yours, special to you.

"Jones," she said.

"Jones," he repeated. "Earl Jones's daughter?"

Earl was what they decided to first-name Daddy.

"Yes," she said.

"Christ." He wiped his hand over his mouth again, then looked behind him. "I'm Jess Taylor. Your dad may have told you about me."

Daddy hadn't said anything about anybody, at least not to her.

"Have you seen him lately? Your dad? I have some things for him."

Tears filled her eye, then her face—her human face formed on top of her skin.

Jess Taylor's expression froze, then he smiled, even though the smile didn't look real.

She wanted to wipe the tear from her eye, but she didn't have hands. One started to form, and she willed it away. She had to stay small.

"You haven't seen him, have you?" Jess Taylor said.

"Not for a long time."

Jess nodded. Then he frowned. He slid out from under the desk, and sat up straight. She squinched to the edge of the box. He was looking at the windows, and now that he thought she couldn't see him, he looked scared.

"What's going on?" she asked.

"I think they're coming back," he said. "We have to move you. Can you stay quiet?"

She had stayed quiet until he asked questions. But she didn't say that. Instead, she said, "Yes."

"I'm going to cover the box. Don't do anything till I come for you. Okay?"

"Okay," she said, even though she was supposed to do two things. She was supposed to stay quiet, and she was supposed to hide.

Maybe when "they" came back, they would bring Momma. Maybe when "they" came back, she could finally go home.

NOW

BECCA AND JILLIAN USED POLICE TAPE to rope off the Natatorium. The crime scene squad could handle the upper floors. Becca saw no point. She knew that the body—the body that was freshly dead—was in that dugout pool.

Jillian was in the basement of the Nat, laying out a grid to work the scene. She knew that some of the work would come from the local team. Even though she had been on the phone with the state crime lab, she had no idea when the experts would show up.

The sooner the better, she had told them, but both she and Becca knew that would make no difference. Oregon was a low tax state, and rather than fund important services, Oregon cut them. The lab was now working two years out on important cases, and had no extra people to spare for a mass grave deep in the desert.

The lab certainly didn't have the funds to hire an expert. Becca would have to take the money from the police budget or she would have to get the Hopewell County

District Attorney to pay for the expert before any charges were filed.

Jillian's office certainly didn't have the money either. She barely had enough funds for an assistant.

Even though other officers showed up, as well as two more detectives, Becca handled most of the interviews herself. She didn't want her colleagues scaring off the illegals. She needed them for the investigation.

Using a mixture of English and her high school Spanish, she managed to interview the work crew. She also learned that several employees had vanished when Chase stopped work and called her, even though he had told them that they'd be safe.

Of course, no one would give her their names. The handful of employees who'd even mentioned their friends seemed frightened by the slip.

Even the legal citizens—the ones who had citizenship, and the ones who were born in the United States—insisted on showing her their papers. A number of the men slapped the documents with their hands, and said, "Test them. Go see. Everything is in order."

When she finished, she went to her car, got some more bottled water, and took a long drink. Yes, the heat had drained her, as had the bodies and the destruction below, but the fear she'd encountered had stressed her as well.

People shouldn't be afraid to answer simple questions. Not in America.

She sighed, then drank half a bottle. She set the bottle inside, shielded her eyes, and looked at the sun.

It seemed to have a long way to go before it disappeared behind the mountains. Usually she liked the long days of summer. Today she didn't.

"Can I send everyone home now?" Chase asked from behind her.

"Yeah." She didn't turn around. She hated his habit of standing so close that she would have to bump into him if she made any movement at all. "Unfortunately, they're not going to be able to work here tomorrow."

"Or the next day or the next. What's this about experts?"

"Jillian can't handle the site," Becca said. "She thinks it's historical, and if she does something wrong…"

He sighed. She knew he understood historical red tape. He had to deal with a lot of it just to get this project off the ground.

"What else do you need from me?" he asked.

I need you to back up a little, she thought. But she said, "I need to see the rest of the buildings. Are any of them locked?"

"A few," he said. "Mostly the theater, which is where I've been storing supplies, and of course, the hotel."

He had stepped into her line of sight, apparently annoyed at the way she had been ignoring him. Since he was no longer so close, she could turn.

"The hotel?" she asked. "Why the hotel? We all went in it as kids."

"And had no idea how much the front desk or the doorknobs were worth. I've got a lot of subcontractors here, and it's a different time." He ran a hand through his hair. Sweat glistened on some of the strands. "I'm going to lose it all, aren't I?"

She felt a pull of empathy. "I don't know. You will be able to work here again. I'm just not sure when."

He gave her a bitter smile. "Yeah."

She wanted to ask him if he regretted calling her. She wanted to ask if he was going to blame her for the loss of time.

But she didn't. The old Becca would have asked those questions.

The new Becca had to pretend she didn't care.

THEN

JESS TAYLOR PICKED UP THE BOX and carried it under his arm. It bumped as he walked. She lost her mouth and one of the eyes as more shivers ran through her.

She wondered: If she thought of herself as Sarah, would she change into a little human girl?

She wasn't willing to try it. Not yet.

He set her next to a filing cabinet. The grained wood reminded her of her father. He'd turned into an expensive filing cabinet once, just to show her how to change into common business objects.

For an emergency, he had said. *For an emergency.*

Like this one. If she had thought it through, she should have turned into something freestanding like the filing cabinet, not something long and seemingly never-ending, like the sidewalk or the bricks.

It was different to become a permanent non-breathing object. Then she had to cling to it, and somehow sleep. But younglins couldn't do that. It was a skill they got when they grew older.

At her age, only a parent could help her make a sleep-change.

Jess Taylor dropped a towel over the box. The towel smelled of soap and sweat. It filtered the light.

She closed her remaining eye, and listened as voices filled the bank. Excited voices, male—

"What the hell were you thinking staying here?"

"You missed it all."

"You should've seen it. They didn't even look human by the end."

The voices mingled and tumbled and twisted into jumbles of words. But *they didn't even look human* got repeated over and over again.

They didn't look human, her people. Not when they were filing cabinets or chairs or wooden sidewalk planks. But they breathed and fought and *thought*. Wasn't that enough?

Daddy had said it would be, that day so long ago:

We have no choice, he'd said to the assembled. *We're stuck here, and Hope is better than the other cities I've seen. We're isolated. If we can work our way into their minds as laborers, maybe they'll accept us. They can't see how we live—we'll have to live as they do. But after a while, they'll get used to us. They'll see how similar we are. We breathe like them, fight like them, think like them. They'll understand. They'll accept. Given time.*

Time passed. And nothing changed. They had their own part of town, near the Chinese who also refused to talk to them.

And when one of their own got attacked outside of town and couldn't hold her shape—

Well, Momma wouldn't talk about it. And everyone expected Daddy to do something, but he didn't know what to do. He told Momma that. He didn't know.

Then he left. Looking for someplace new, Momma said. But she didn't believe it any more. Daddy would have come back long before now. And he hadn't.

And Jess Taylor looked sad when he learned her human name. Because of Daddy.

The voices continued:

"They scream real pretty though."

"One of them even begged."

"You shoulda been there."

And then Jess Taylor said, "Someone had to watch the bank."

"If I didn't know better," said a deep male voice, "I'd check the vault. What a perfect time to take something for yourself."

"Please do, sir," Jess Taylor said. "You won't find anything awry."

He sounded funny. Like they'd hurt his feelings. Humans did that to each other sometimes. But they always made up. Never with her people, but with each other.

Only no one apologized to Jess Taylor. Instead, the conversations changed. Someone walked past her and she heard a dial spin, then something metal click. She swiveled her good eye, but she couldn't see through that towel Jess Taylor had thrown over her box.

"Looks fine to me, sir," said another voice.

"Double-check," said the deep voice.

"I don't receive credit for staying, do I?" Jess Taylor asked in that low tone he'd used when he called his own people names.

"What's that?" the deep voice asked.

"Nothing, sir."

More clicking. The sound of boots against marble. Low voices, counting and comparing.

Then deep voice—"Looks like you did well, Taylor."

"Thank you, sir."

"Just don't act on your own again, all right? Makes people suspicious. Especially in these times."

"Do you think I'm one of them, sir?"

"If you were, you'd be dumb to stay," deep voice said.

"Besides," said another voice, "we seen you hurt. You don't change like those demons do."

"I suppose," Jess Taylor said in that low tone again.

"You don't approve," said the other voice.

"Of what?" Jess Taylor asked, louder this time.

"What we done."

For a long moment, Jess Taylor didn't answer. She held her breath, hoping he wouldn't make a mistake. If he made a mistake, they would find her.

Finally, he said, "I don't know what you did."

"We could show you," one of the men said, and everyone laughed.

"Thank you," Jess Taylor said without any warmth, "but I think I can figure it out for myself."

NOW

THE FRONT DOOR OF THE HOTEL WAS PADLOCKED. The window shutters were closed and locked as well. When she was a child, this looked like an abandoned building, spooky but still alive. Now it seemed like an un-loved place, a place that would fall apart if someone took the locks off.

Becca watched Chase remove the padlock and hook it onto his belt. Then he swung back the metal latch and pushed open the double mahogany doors.

Those Becca remembered. She remembered the way that the light filtered out through them, more dust motes than she thought possible dancing inside of it.

Small windows stood beside the door, but on the far side of the lobby, floor-to-ceiling windows opened onto the expanse of high desert and the mountains beyond. The glass was old and bubbled and clearly handmade. Such dramatic windows were rare a hundred years ago, and had been—in the hotel's heyday—one of its main drawing points.

She stepped inside, sneezed at the smells of mold and dust, and watched as more motes swirled because of her movements. Chase stood beside the door, watching her.

"We were going to revive it all," he said. The past tense saddened her. "Imagine that desk over there, polished, with employees behind it, computers on top, guests in front."

She looked at the registration desk, scratched and filthy, which wrapped around an entire corner of the room. Behind it were old-fashioned mail slots, some filled with stuffing from chairs—probably rats' or mice nests.

"People would look at the view, or go to the Natatorium for tennis or a swim. We were going to build a golf course alongside this, and build homes, just outside the line of sight for these windows." Chase stuck his hands in his back pockets. He stared at the view, still sending in light despite the dirty glass. "It would have been spectacular."

"It's not over yet, Chase," Becca said. It wasn't like him to give up so easily. In fact, this speech of his was making her suspicious. Had he run into financial difficulty? Had he put something recently dead among the bones as a way of notifying the authorities? Did he want the project to end for a reason she didn't understand yet?

"Half my crew probably ran away today."

"They aren't the people who will restore this building."

"Who's going to come once they find out there's a mass grave on the property?"

She didn't know the answer to that. "People go to battlefields all the time."

"Battlefields," he said, "are different."

"We went to Little Big Horn. They're still discovering bodies up there."

"From a hundred and forty years ago," he said.

"You have no idea how old these bodies are," she said.

He shrugged, then turned and gave her one of his "aw-what-the-hell" smiles. "You're right. I don't know anything yet. Except that this place was well named."

The End of the World. She sighed, and asked the question she'd suddenly started to dread. "Are you insured?"

"For what? Construction losses? Sure. Lost income and disability? Sure. Dead bodies on my construction site? Who the hell knows."

"Maybe you should find out," she said. "I'm sure this doesn't qualify as an act of God."

He inclined his head toward her, as if to say "Touché."

"I need to look," she said. "Alone."

He nodded, then walked to the door. "Find me when you're done."

"Yeah," she said, but he had already stepped outside. She sighed and looked at the floor. Dirt covered the old carpet. Footprints ran through it, some of them so old that they were buried under layers of sand. Broken chairs huddled in the corner, and the stairs to the second floor had rotted away.

But the hotel did have good bones. The brick on the outside had insulated it from harsh weather in the high desert—the hot, hot summers and the blisteringly cold winters. Even the floor-to-ceiling windows were double paned, something so unusual, she'd never seen it in a building this old.

The place didn't smell of death like the Natatorium. In fact, except for her prints and Chase's it didn't look like anyone had been here in a month or more.

She turned on her flashlight and aimed it at the dark corners. Something skittered away from the ornate gold leaf in front of the elevator. She scanned the steps—yep, rotted—and the scarred reception desk. A door was open behind it, leading to the offices. She'd been back there when she was a kid.

In fact, she'd been everywhere in this place as a child. The whole hotel had fascinated her, except for one part.

She steeled herself, then moved to the right, aiming the light at the far wall. When the beam hit it, the wallpaper shimmered like a heat mirage.

She swallowed. That, at least, hadn't changed. The shimmering wall and the building moans—probably from the way the wind whistled through it on dry desert days—gave rise to the stories of the hotel being haunted.

A shiver ran through her. She'd just seen a hole filled with long-dead bodies, her nose still carried the odor of decay (and her clothing probably did too), and it was the old hotel that scared her out of her wits.

Let someone else investigate it. Let the crime scene techs make sure nothing bad had happened here in the recent past. She'd done as much as she was going to.

She shut off her light, and tried not to listen to the rustling as she let herself out.

THEN

AFTER A LONG LONG TIME, most of the voices stopped. A few continued. Deep Voice did. He gave orders and talked to some of the others.

Then he told Jess Taylor to leave.

She held her breath, wondering what would happen to her.

Then someone picked up the box. She bumped against the side.

"What've you got there?" Deep Voice asked.

"Just a box," Jess Taylor said. "I need to move a few things from my house. I thought I'd take this to pack them in. I'll bring it back in the morning."

"Check it, Dunnigan," Deep Voice said.

She shivered. She couldn't help herself. She squinched as far as she could into the corner of the box, turned her ear inward, and closed her remaining eye, hoping this Dunnigan couldn't see her—or if he did, he wouldn't know what he was looking at.

The box bounced, then the light changed. The towel must have come off. Tobacco and sweat filled the air.

She held herself rigid, feeling a shiver start, and willing it away.

"It's empty, boss," said this Dunnigan, right above her.

The box bumped again, and the light dimmed.

"Satisfied?" Jess Taylor asked. His tone was bitter.

"You got to admit," Deep Voice said, "you've been acting odd today."

"I acted like a responsible employee," Jess Taylor said. "I stayed when everyone else left. No one thought to lock up in all the excitement. I made sure the drawers were closed and locked, the safe was closed, and the account registers were in the proper desks. I kept an eye on the place, and you treat me like a criminal."

"You'd do the same, Taylor," Deep Voice said.

"No, sir, I beg your pardon, but I wouldn't. I would acknowledge when an employee does well, not suspect him of thievery because he takes an initiative."

The silence went on forever. She was still holding her breath. She had to let it out, as quietly as she could. She could feel the box bounce with Jess Taylor's breathing—if he was the one holding it. She hoped he was.

He seemed like the only human—the only person—she could trust.

Finally, Deep Voice said, "You can keep the box."

"Thank you, sir." Such sarcasm in Jess Taylor's voice. She wondered if Deep Voice could hear it. "May I go now?"

"Of course," Deep Voice said.

The box bounced with each step. She heard a door screech open, then bang closed. The air grew warmer and the towel blew up ever so slightly.

"Stay still," Jess Taylor said in that undertone of his. "We're not out of this yet."

NOW

WHEN SHE CAME OUT OF THE HOTEL, the sky was a deep grayish blue. Twilight had fallen fast, like it always did on the high desert. The moment the sun dipped behind the mountain peaks, the light changed and the air had a suggestion of coolness.

Now if only the wind would stop. It rose for a half-hour or so at real twilight, sending sand pellets against her skin like tiny knives.

Chase's employees had already left. So had the police, except for two officers who had been assigned to guard the crime scene. Apparently the crime scene techs weren't going to work at night, which made sense, given the location and the questions still lingering about how to handle the scene.

Chase leaned against his Ford Bronco, a cell phone pressed against his ear. His back was to her, but she could tell from the position of his shoulders how annoyed he was.

She walked toward him, then stopped when she heard what he was saying.

"…I'm not sure what they're going to find here, Lester, but that's not the point. The point is that this project probably won't go forward for months. I need you to check our liability. I also need you to examine the insurance policies, and to somehow, without tipping our hand, talk to the few investors who came on board early. I'd promised them the chance of a return within two years. This project came alive because I thought we could fast-track it."

He was talking to his lawyer. Usually such conversations had lawyer-client privilege, but she wasn't sure about that when he conducted it outside on a cell phone.

Still, she should let him know she was there.

She didn't move.

"That's not the point, Lester. The point is that I already have 1.2 million dollars in capital tied up in this place, and now everything's going to be on hold—."

One of the officers saw her. She nodded at him.

"That's why I want you to find out if we're insured for something like this. I'm not sure I can afford to have that much money tied up indefinitely."

She scraped her foot against the dirt as she walked forward again. He continued talking, so she coughed.

He turned, paused, and sighed. Then he said, "Listen, I'll call you in a few hours. Have some answers for me by then, will you?"

"How's Lester?" she asked.

"You heard that?"

"Enough to know who you were talking to." Lester had handled their divorce. He had been Chase's lawyer for more than two decades. She had no idea if he was any good, but Chase obviously had no complaints. He usually fired people who didn't perform their jobs well.

Chase stuck his phone into the front pocket of his shirt. Then he took the padlock off his belt. "I suppose this is the wrong time to ask you to dinner."

"It's always the wrong time, Chase," she said.

He shook his head ever so slightly. "What did I do, Becca? Was being married to me that bad?"

"I divorced you," she said. "That should be answer enough."

But it wasn't, because he asked her often. And he made it sound like she had been crazy to leave him. Which, her therapist said, was proof enough to her that she had done the right thing.

Becca waited until he'd padlocked the hotel before she walked to her squad. Even then, she stood with an arm resting on the open door as he walked back to his Bronco.

He looked defeated. Was Chase a good enough actor to play such a difficult emotion? She wasn't sure, but she doubted it.

And Jillian would say that she doubted it because she wanted to.

"Changed my mind," Becca said when he got close. "How's pizza sound to you?"

"Good if they had the real thing here."

He'd gone to school in Chicago; he thought the pizza out west was too mainstream or too California. Tasteless and low-fat, he'd once said.

She expected the response, just not the rote way he said it.

"Well, how about that thing we call pizza out here in the wild, wild west?"

He looked at her for the longest time as if he were sizing her up. She made sure her expression remained neutral.

"You going to interrogate me?" he asked.

"Should I?"

"I suppose you should." He opened the Bronco's door. "And you should know I'm ordering spaghetti."

"Spoilsport," she said, got into the squad, and followed Chase out of the lot.

THEN

THE BOX BOUNCED for what seemed like forever. She heard boots tapping on the wooden sidewalk, boots scraping on dirt, boots going silent as they hit the grass. She heard voices, conversations far from her. She heard a motorized engine, one of those new-fangled automobiles that made humans think they had entered a technological age.

Daddy had always said they were backwards. If they were just a bit farther along, if the Earth hadn't been so focused on oil and gas and coal, then maybe their people could have rebuilt the ship. But the materials hadn't been manufactured yet, and the energy sources were too heavy or too combustible. The people needed something more sophisticated, but didn't have the resources to make it themselves.

Nor did they have the ability to take what passed for technology in this place and modify it for their needs.

Occasionally one of the voices would greet Jess Taylor and ask him what he had in the box. He'd give the same reply—*Nothing*—and continue as if that were true.

He walked for a long time.

Then she heard boots on wood again, a few creaks, and the click of a doorknob. Another creak—this one different, like a door opening—and the light filtering through the towel seemed dimmer.

Finally, Jess Taylor set the box down.

"Just a minute," he said.

She heard a door close, then a swish that she recognized—curtains being closed. This place was hot. The windows should've been open instead of covered. The air smelled faintly of grease and unwashed sheets

Then the towel came off. She swiveled her eye upwards. Jess Taylor was looking down at her.

"This is my house," he said. "I live alone, so no one'll bother us. I don't have to be anywhere until tomorrow."

She wasn't sure why he was telling her all that.

He scooted a chair closer to the table, sat down, then asked, "Do you have any idea what we should do next?"

NOW

Becca didn't have to tell him where they were going because there was only one pizza parlor in all of Hope that he would step into. It was in a beat-up old building on the southeast side, about as far from the End of the World as they could go.

The pizza parlor—called Reuben's of all things—was actually owned by a displaced New York Italian who missed his grandmother's cooking. He made pizza because teenagers loved it and because it was a cheap, easy meal for families, but his heart was in the Italian dishes, from lasagna to a special homemade sausage marinara whose recipe he kept secret.

Chase came out of the bathroom as she went into the ladies room. When she came out, Chase was sitting toward the back, in a red vinyl booth, his hands folded on the checked tablecloth. The edges of his hair were wet as was one side of his face.

Washing up hadn't entirely gotten rid of the smell of rot that had permeated her nose, but it got knocked back a degree. The rich odor of garlic and baking bread helped.

By the time she got to the table, Chase was sipping a glass of wine. An iced tea waited for her. Irritation flooded through her—how did he know what she wanted? Had he asked? No, of course not—and then she shook it off.

He had always done this, and until she left him, she had let him. She hadn't told him in any way that he no longer had the right to make decisions for her, and now didn't seem the time.

"I ordered the family-sized spaghetti with the sausage marinara," he said.

She sighed. She was going to have to confront him after all.

But he held up his hand, as if to forestall anything she had to say.

"Then I realized I was being a jerk, so I ordered a small pepperoni pizza and a basket of garlic bread."

As he said that, the garlic bread arrived, looking crisp and greasy and delicious.

"Sorry. I know I should know better."

Becca wasn't sure if that was a real apology or not. She wasn't even sure she should be annoyed or not. Sometimes she wished her therapist was on speed-dial, so she could ask a simple question: What was the appropriate response to this particular Chase action? Should she be flattered or insulted? Should she set him in his place? Or should she do her breathing exercises while she reminded herself that they were no longer married?

"We could, I think, change the topping on the pizza." He actually sounded worried. "I don't think it went into the oven yet."

"No, that's fine," she said. "A hundred-thousand fat-filled calories actually sound good right now."

So she had opted onto a response, and it was passive/aggressive. Bully for her. How non-constructive.

Chase blinked, looking a little stunned, then shrugged. "Sounds like you're in the mood to interrogate me."

Becca grabbed a slice of garlic bread. The butter welled against her fingers, and she realized she was hungry.

"How much do you stand to lose if the End of the World folds?"

"Folds?" he asked. "Or gets put on hold?"

"It's the same thing, isn't it? Didn't you tell me you needed to finish this quick?"

He swirled his wine glass, then took a huge swig, something she'd never seen him do.

"Let me explain the End of the World, can I, before we get into the details you think important?"

She wasn't the only one capable of being passive/aggressive, but she let the comment slide. She had baited him, after all.

"Shoot," she said.

He flagged the waiter down, got them both water, and drank his so quickly that he looked like a man dying of thirst. Then he pushed his other glass toward the back of the table, as if saving the wine for later.

"The End of the World," he said, the words rolling off his tongue like a lover's. "Remember how much we loved it?"

How much he had loved it. But she didn't correct him. She nodded instead.

"Remember when I used to talk about restoring it, about making the End of the World *the* destination resort in Oregon, and you'd laugh, and you'd say who would want to come to Hope?"

"That was before the boom," she said, surprised that she wasn't feeling defensive.

"Before Hollywood discovered how cheap the land was, before they filmed half the Western films up here, before the Californians bought everything in sight."

And tried to change the town into a mini-California, with its strip malls and coffee bars and upscale shops that people like Becca couldn't set foot into unless there was a police emergency.

"Hollywood's left," she said. "They've gone to Canada."

"But they vacation here. They ski, they hunt, they fish. They look at the pretty views. They want to play golf and lacrosse and polo and soccer, if we could only accommodate them. The town doesn't have everything yet, and if we did, even more would come."

"Is this the speech you gave to prospective investors?" she asked. "Because I know the drill."

He'd practiced much of it on her over the years. She hadn't agreed with all of it, but she had encouraged some of it. She too wanted Hope to grow. When she'd been a girl, the town was dying, and the name seemed like the way the town planned for its future.

"Historic resorts are the next travel boom," he said. "People want to visit the past, so long as it has all the amenities of the present."

The waiter set down the pizza. The cheese was still popping because the tomato sauce was bubbling underneath.

Becca took a piece. To her surprise, Chase did too.

"So tell me," she said, "how come your money's in this instead of other people's?"

He sighed. "It costs more to refurbish the old hotel and the Natatorium than it would to tear the place down, and build comparable modern buildings from scratch."

"And your investors didn't like that?"

"They like everything else. They like the resort, the golf courses—

"Courses?" Becca asked.

"Four," he said, "along with residential housing, riding trails, and a possible dude ranch near the edge of the mountains."

"How much property did you buy?"

"Just the End of the World," he said. "Turns out that the property runs from the highway all the way to the mountains."

"My god," Becca said.

"It was all scrub and desert, not even good enough for ranching, although the End of the World's original owners did rent it out for that."

"Who did you buy it from?" she asked.

"The heirs. They don't live in Oregon any longer. They remembered it from their childhoods, figured the land wasn't worth much, and sold it for a song. The land wasn't the problem. The hotel and resort were."

"The investors wanted you to build new, and you refused." Her voice rose just a bit at the end of the statement, mostly because she was surprised. Chase did what he wanted within reason, but he never turned down money like this. "You really had your heart set on rebuilding the place."

"I had documents and itineraries and research and projections that showed just how much people would love it here. They go to historic lodges now. Hell, Timberline Resort is the number two destination in Oregon."

"Number one being?"

He looked down. "Spirit Mountain Casino."

Which had no historic hotel. Nothing except a rather cheap looking lodge and a large casino at the entrance to the Van Duzer Corridor in the coastal mountain range.

"But that land was considered worthless forty years ago," he said.

"Because it was tribal land in the middle of nowhere," she said.

"You don't have to side with them," he snapped.

The reaction shocked her. He never snapped. He got angry or frustrated and occasionally raised his voice, but usually he manipulated, twisting the conversation until she was surprised that she was agreeing with him, even when she knew she shouldn't.

"So I repeat," she said, "how deep are you into this?"

"Ninety percent of the resort funding is from me." He took another swig of the wine, leaving the glass nearly empty. How many times had he told her wine was meant to be sipped not guzzled? He probably hadn't even tasted this one.

"That's a lot of money."

"More than you realize."

"So you go bankrupt if this place never gets off the ground."

He finished the wine, then set the glass at the edge of the table, an obvious signal for more. "You're awful damn pessimistic."

"I'm not pessimistic, and I'm not here to judge you." Even though that was a lie. At this moment, it was her job to judge him. "I am trying to figure out what happened in that Natatorium."

"You think someone murdered a lot of people and buried them beneath the swimming pool. A long, long time ago. I think it shouldn't interfere with my project."

She sighed. "I'm not talking about the old bodies. I'm talking about the smell."

He froze. The waiter returned, grabbed the wine glass, and left without asking what he was supposed to do about Chase's beverage. Maybe the look on Chase's face scared him off.

"I told you," Chase said. "It was an animal."

"We haven't found it yet. We're operating on the assumption that the recent body is human."

"And you think I what? Sabotaged my own project? Why the hell would I do that?"

"I don't know." Becca raised her voice enough to drown his out. "Maybe you don't have enough funding. Maybe you want out now."

"And you think that destroying the project is the way to leave? If I want to lose several million dollars, I'd put it on the roulette table. If I want to shut down the project, I'll do that."

"So why didn't you?"

"I didn't want to." He grabbed the edge of the table. For a moment, she thought he was going to leverage himself out of it.

But he didn't. He ran a hand through his hair, took a deep breath, and forced himself to lean back.

"You don't want to?" she asked. "Or you see this as a win-win situation?"

He looked at her as if she was crazy. "Excuse me?"

"Once you found the bodies below the pool, you knew that might stall the project. But you wanted out without losing any money. So you found a way that the insurance might cover it. Something guaranteed, not an ancient burial ground like you thought, but a police investigation—"

"You think I planted a body there for the *insurance money*?"

"I don't know," she said. "Did you?"

His mouth was open. He stared at her like the day she told him she was leaving. If she had to, she would wager that he was telling the truth. But those kinds of experiences, that kind of hunch, didn't hold up in court.

Besides, she knew that her reactions to him weren't always the right ones.

"Do you really think that little of me?" he asked softly.

"What I think doesn't matter," she said. "This *is* a police investigation, and I have to—"

"Oh, bullshit," he said. "You don't have to explore every goddamn angle. You think I'm capable of killing someone and planting him in the Natatorium for the fucking insurance money."

The waiter hovered near the kitchen door. In his hand, he held another glass of wine. He watched them with a wary expression.

She had to get Chase to calm down. She needed him to think clearly.

"Do you want me to investigate this or someone from Portland? Because that's the way it's heading."

"Even if I turn out to be right and it's a goddamn coyote down there?"

"Even if," she said. "We have something big now, and there's no covering it up. Jillian called the state crime lab. We're going to have reporters. You want them to write about how we had a screaming fight in our favorite Italian restaurant?"

"Fuck you, Becca," he said. "You planned this."

"Your anger?'

"With a fucking audience. Do you hate me that much?"

She swallowed. She was getting angry now. "You ask me that a lot. So here's the answer, Chase. I don't hate you. If anything, I'm still in love with your sorry ass, and that's a problem for me. It's also a problem for this investigation, since I'm the only trained detective on Hope's police force. I'm holding off the Valley investigative team for the moment, but that won't last if we keep this up."

He slammed his hands on the booth so hard that the fake wood tabletop attached to the wall actually bounced. Then he stood up and stalked to the men's room.

Becca took a deep breath, let it out, and then took another. And another, and another, still wishing for the therapist on speed-dial. Did she keep breathing until she was light-headed or did she just leave?

She was handling this all wrong, and pretty soon word would get out. The chief would relieve her, and the investigation would become a state thing instead of a local thing. And that kind of publicity would hurt the new Hope, the place that actually had a future.

The waiter came to the table. He was still cradling the wine glass. "You think he's gonna want this? Because—"

"Yeah," she said. "He'll want that and more. Bring the whole bottle."

She ate her piece of pizza slowly, drank the iced tea, and waited, keeping an eye on the men's room door. The three other tables, filled with young families, kept an eye on her, as if she had been the problem, not Chase.

The men's room door opened as she finished her third piece. The waiter had been back twice—once with the wine bottle and once with a heaping bowl of spaghetti in sausage marina sauce. As stressed as Becca was, she could probably eat the entire thing without Chase's help.

To her relief, he came back to the booth and slid in.

"Okay," he said, "since you're going all official on me, here's what you need to know. I have six million dollars into this thing. That's real money. I also have outstanding loans of ten million, and that's not nearly enough to get everything done. I'm hoping when the hotel and Nat are finished, the investors will pour in. If they don't, I'll be in debt until I die, even if the place is a success."

Becca set down the pizza crust she'd been clinging to. She resisted the urge to slide the plate of spaghetti toward her.

"Does my insurance cover this? How the hell would I know? I'm sure my agent doesn't know. I'm sure the insurance company has no real idea, and its legal department will be haggling over the policy language and the politics of the entire thing for months. That's what I was talking to Lester about. I'm hoping that he can find a few answers, or at least an argument, so that some of the back and forth gets forestalled if and when you people actually decide to shut me down."

"We already shut you down, Chase," she said. "The question now is for how long."

"I know." He picked up the glass and then set it down again. "But you know what I mean. This could be a two-day inconvenience or it could be a year-long nightmare. And since it's all one property, I'm pretty sure that you could tie me up for a long time."

"If those bodies are Native American, you could be right," she said.

He let out a long sigh. Then he moved the wine glass closer to her plate than his.

"So," he said, "do I have a motive to get insurance money? No. I'd be a fool to try this plan. If I wanted insurance money, I'd find another way to go about it. And I'd be smart, Becca. This is damn dumb. It jeopardizes everything without giving me any benefit at all. I'll be in the news forever, I won't be able to save face, and I'm going to go broke. Hell, I'd be better off disappearing and starting all over again than doing that. I'm not damn dumb, Becca."

"I know," she said.

"I have no reason to plant something there."

"Does anyone else?" she asked.

"Yeah," he said, reaching for the plate of spaghetti. "Yeah, I'm afraid a lot of people do."

THEN

Why would he ask her what to do next? Wasn't he the grown one, the one in charge? She was just a baby, really, younger than anyone else in their group.

But he wasn't part of their group. She wasn't even sure there was a group any more. Where had everyone gone?

When the shanties burned, the remaining people fled. Momma had grabbed her. They were just a little behind the group.

And she never knew what happened to any of them.

"What about my Momma?" she asked Jess Taylor.

He closed his eyes, turned his head, and wiped the sweat off his forehead. Then he glanced at the window, like he wanted to open it. He stood, and she thought he was going to, but all he did was get another towel and clean off his fingers.

When he sat back down, his face had a different look to it. His eyes were open, but sadder, if that was possible.

Sometimes she wondered how these humans could think themselves so different from the people. These humans changed too, just not as much. And sometimes these humans changed by force of will, just like the people did.

Just like Jess Taylor had done a moment ago.

"You're going to keep asking, aren't you?" he said.

She blinked at him. She didn't know how to answer, except maybe to say of course she would. She loved her momma and her momma left her on the sidewalk.

Bad things happened this afternoon, and she heard some of them. One of them sounded like Momma.

"I don't know what happened," he said. "I'll find out as best I can. I promise. But it might take days."

Days. She wanted to fold her ears in, close her eyes, and huddle into a little ball. What would happen to her for those days?

"I've seen this before," he said. "Not this, exactly, but the same kind of thing. Folks get riled up about the strangest things, and you have to admit, your people are strange."

She didn't think so. But she didn't answer that either, just kept watching him.

"I mean, I think I finally understand where this violence comes from, this impulse. Not because of you."

He held up a hand, as if to reassure her. She wasn't sure what he was reassuring her about.

"It comes about because of the differences. They're startling. And sometimes—I don't mean to offend you—but sometimes, they're revolting. Humans don't handle revulsion well. We…."

He shook his head and stood up, walking to the window, and peeking through the curtain. Sweat stained the back of his shirt, leaving a V-shaped wet spot in the fabric.

"I can't believe I'm defending them."

He shook his head again. Then he let the curtain drop close, and he came back to the chair.

"The chances are—I'm so sorry, but the chances are that your mother didn't make it. Just like your father. She probably—they probably—I mean, you heard it this afternoon. You're lucky to be here. And if your mother is alive—"

He stopped, wiped a hand over his mouth, then shook his head yet again.

He didn't say any more.

She was holding her breath. She finally let it out. Her other eye had appeared. Apparently she needed to see him. Her body was starting to make changes on its own.

"You think she's still alive?" she asked.

"No," he said.

"But you said—"

"I know what I said." He sighed. "Look, Sarah, if your mother is still alive, it probably won't be for long."

"Then we have to find her."

"That's not what I mean."

She felt her skin tighten. Another shiver ran through her. The spikes started to form and she willed them away. She didn't want him to know she suddenly felt threatened.

"What do you mean?" she asked.

"I mean they're probably not done."

"But I heard the men, they came into the bank, they said it was over, they said it was…fun…. They said—"

"I know what they said." He ran his fingers along his forehead. "I know. And I know a few of them will go back. Some probably haven't left. And they'll finish. Do you understand me? They'll finish."

"Can't we get her before they do?"

He stared at her, and that sadness returned to his eyes. His whole face looked sad, and she wondered for a minute if he even saw her, if he was looking at her or something else—someone else—like a memory, maybe, like those ghostly shapes that the people sometimes made when they thought of a relative long dead.

"If we try to get her," he said, "they'll kill us too."

"Not you," she said.

He let out half a laugh, like she'd startled the sound out of him.

"Sarah, honey," he said, "if your people hadn't come, they'd've gotten to me eventually. They always do."

NOW

"YOU KNOW WHO DOESN'T LIKE ME." Chase used tongs to dish up his spaghetti. Somehow he managed to do so without getting sauce on his shirt. "You used to put up with the phone calls."

Becca remembered. The calls came in late at night. Sometimes they were just hang-ups. Sometimes they were more serious than that. A few even included threats.

In those days, Hope's telephone system was too unsophisticated to provide services like Caller I.D., so Becca had had to put a trace on the line. She had gone to every single one of the callers, warning them that their behavior was illegal and should Chase's businesses go under or should he get hurt, they would be the first suspects she went to.

Most seemed to listen. A few grumbled that Chase had only married her because he wanted police protection. Not even Becca was insecure enough to believe that.

She took a small portion of the spaghetti, barely enough to fill a corner of the plate provided, and then only because she loved the sauce. Mostly, she focused on the pizza, her iced tea, and Chase.

"What about this project?" she asked. "Anyone new surface?"

He used his spoon as a counterweight to keep the spaghetti he was winding from falling off his fork. He worked at it as if it were a particularly difficult puzzle.

"Obviously, you never went to the city council meetings."

"Not for this, no," she said. She avoided city business as much as possible.

"Half the town hated it. Some I didn't expect, folks who had supported me when I wanted to redo Beiker's Department Store downtown."

"The preservationists went against you?"

"Yeah." He ate the forkful, swallowed, and then drank some water. "They think the End of the World is a bad idea, a dangerous place, and the last straw in turning Hope into a replica of California."

"Wow," Becca said. "I'd've thought they would've loved it."

"Me, too," he said. "I was stunned. A few actually threatened me."

"You're kidding."

He shook his head. "Ray McGuillicuty, remember him? He told me I'd regret buying the End of the World."

"You think that was a threat, coming from a 90-year-old man?"

Chase shrugged. "I thought it was idle talk at the time. But he has money, connections, and a shady reputation. He made his money running illegal speakeasies in the late

'30s, and gambling dens in the '40s. Word around town was that if there was an illegal business—an abortionist, a fight ring, drug smuggling—McGuillicuty would rent space or manpower to that business for a cut, of course."

She had heard the rumors, but she also knew Old Man McGuillicuty had been an upstanding citizen since the 1960s.

"You think he's still got that kind of pull?"

"I think if anyone in Hope is smart enough to stop my project by burying a body on the property, it's Ray Mc-Guillicuty."

"That's giving him a lot of power."

"If you're right," Chase said, "and someone is trying to shut me down, Ray's my first choice."

Becca tried not to laugh. She couldn't imagine that old man caring so much about the future of Hope. But she wasn't going to ignore this.

"Who else?" she asked as she finished her iced tea. She waved the glass at the waiter, and he nodded.

"Oh, Christ," Chase said. "Damn near the entire preservation society. All the matrons and their husbands too. Most of the old money in Hope—what there is of it— warned me away."

"Like Old Man McGuillicuty did?" Becca asked. The waiter showed up with a pitcher and set it on the table. He didn't even bother to pour. He still seemed a bit nervous about Chase's earlier outburst.

"Not that blatant," Chase said. "But they all took time to tell me that the End of the World is the most unlucky place in Hope and that everyone connected to it has been harmed by that connection."

"Lovely," Becca said. "Superstition still alive and well."

"And apparently they thought I should make business decisions based on it."

"You didn't, though," she said.

"I think some of my investors did," he said. "The preservation committee knew who my usual investors were. A number of them were contacted and a few backed out. One even told me that old properties that had bad luck rumors usually had a reason for them."

"Turns out he was right," Becca said.

"She," he said. "And I guess she was."

"Which means…" Becca tapped a finger against her chin. "…that someone knew about those bodies."

"How do you figure?" Chase asked.

She smiled at him. "Bad luck rumors have to start somewhere."

"You think that's tied to the smell?" he asked.

"Probably not, but right now, those old bodies are the only crime I have to investigate. I'll start there."

"After you finish harassing the local businessmen."

"After I finish dinner with my former husband, who has had a hell of a day."

THEN

SHE DIDN'T KNOW WHAT JESS TAYLOR meant by the humans getting to him, and he wouldn't say. He paced around the front part of the cabin, poured some water from a pitcher into a glass, and drank.

Then he stared at her.

She wondered if he was sorry he'd helped her. Maybe he would turn her in.

Maybe she would scream.

She wanted to beg him to keep her, beg him to help her. But she didn't. Daddy used to say that people who begged didn't deserve help. They had to help themselves.

Only she couldn't do that, not without knowing what had happened. The answers weren't simple. Her home was gone—she knew that much. When the shanties burned, hers would've burned with it. Daddy always kept water near the candles. He used to say, *This place is so primitive and so badly built that we're going to die here in a stupid fire because we couldn't get to it in time.*

He'd been wrong about them dying. None of them had died in that cabin, although she wasn't sure about the others, the people who lived in the shanties where the fires started.

She wished Daddy were here now. She wished he would talk to Jess Taylor, grown one to grown one. They would understand each other. They would know what had happened and what would happen next.

"Do you eat?" Jess Taylor asked. He swished the water around in his glass. He was still looking at her that funny way.

She had to form a mouth. She had lost it while he'd been pacing. Her body wasn't sure what form to take so it was taking several at once, which made her dizzy.

"I eat," she said.

"I mean, do you eat what we eat?"

"When I look like you," she said. Her people's food had gone away when she was really, really little. They had to become like the humans just so that they could take in human nourishment.

"When you look like me," Jess Taylor repeated. "How about the way you look now?"

"I'm not anything now," she said. "I need to be something to take in food."

Something she understood. Something whose systems were somewhat compatible. Daddy and the other scientists had to work for a while to make their systems work like a human's. They still had to make changes—changes she didn't understand.

Daddy said she was lucky. She started changing into human form really young, so it would be ingrained. If she had to hide, she could hide as one of them forever because her body was used to their strangeness.

His never would be. Some of the older people got really sick in the first years.

Some of the older people died.

"How often do you have to eat?" Jess Taylor asked.

"I don't know," she said. "Whenever you do, I guess."

Because she always ate when Momma did. She was too young to pick her own times to eat. Eating had to be trained like everything else.

"Wonderful," he said in that low voice of his, the one no one else was supposed to hear. Then he raised it a little. "How about water? Do you need that too?"

"If I look like you," she said, "I act like you. My needs are like yours."

That's the beauty of it, Daddy said to Momma once. *And the curse. If we stay here too long, we lose our identity. We become someone else. Then they'll never find us.*

Why would they look for us? Momma asked. *For all they know, we missed our settlement location and made do.*

They trace new colonies. They have to, Daddy said. *We don't just move there because of population growth. These places are carefully chosen for raw material wealth as well.*

She wasn't sure what "raw material wealth" was, but Momma had known. Momma had looked at Daddy disapprovingly. Daddy had shrugged, because he wore his human all the time now, and then he had smiled at her.

They'll track us down, if only to see what kind of wealth we discovered here.

And if we don't find any? Momma said.

That's not the concern, Daddy said. *The concern is whether not they'll find us before we lose ourselves.*

"So you're going to have to pick a shape sometime tonight, aren't you?" Jess Taylor said. He had moved closer to her. She hadn't noticed before. Had she been so lost in her memories that she hadn't seen him walk?

"I guess," she said.

"Can you be something else for a while? A table, maybe or the box?"

"I'm too little," she said. "I can't do it by myself, not for long. That's why I couldn't be brick. I tried, but I'm not good yet. And I can't stay long anyway. I don't know the sleep-change. I need to move and breathe and feed myself like you."

He sighed. He sank into the chair next to the table. "I was afraid of that."

He took another sip of the water, studied his hand, then studied the small cabin. Then he got up and went to the window again, peering out the curtain.

"No one," he said. "We're okay for now."

"I know," she said, even though she didn't. She wanted him to figure out how to help her. She was becoming more and more afraid he would just throw her out now that he knew most of her secrets.

He put his hand in the box, near her skin but not touching it. "You turned the color of the brick this afternoon," he said. "Can you turn the same color as me?"

She looked at him as hard as he had looked at her. Then she let out a little sigh.

"Yes," she said.

"You sounded hesitant," he said.

"I can't do blue eyes," she said. "Yours aren't."

He smiled suddenly, as if he hadn't expected that. "You're right. Mine aren't. Anything else human you can't do?"

"I can't be a grown one," she said. "I have to 'roughly correspond.'"

She said those last two words carefully. They were Daddy's words. Before she had only known the concept, not how to express it. She used to point to things, things she wanted to be for more than an hour, more than a day.

He would shake his head. Sometimes he would laugh. She loved it when her Daddy laughed.

Younglin, he'd say, *they have to roughly correspond.*

Mostly she wanted to be a grown one. Humans, more than the people, treated their young ones very differently. But she didn't have enough years to be a grown one. She couldn't pretend it, couldn't even get the size right.

That problem translated to other living things as well. She could be a sapling, but not a tree. A kitten, but not a cat.

Someday, she would roughly correspond. But she wouldn't know when until she changed to human form, and that form was a grown one.

"You're a girl," Jess Taylor said, "or they wouldn't call you Sarah. What age do you roughly correspond to?"

"Ten," she said because that's what Momma said when she took her to the school two years before. Even though her learning had grown and her grades had advanced, she hadn't changed, not like her classmates.

So she'd asked Daddy about that, and he'd said, *Roughly, younglin. Roughly correspond. We age differently than they do. Slower, I think.*

But he didn't know. There was so much they didn't know. So much that they didn't understand.

Then he left and no one knew, and Momma hated the questions.

"Ten," Jess Taylor said, and nodded, almost pleased. "Ten might work."

"For what?" she asked, the words catching in her newly formed mouth.

"For keeping you alive, child," he said, and tapped the edge of the box as he stood. "For keeping you alive."

NOW

By the time Becca got home, she was too tired to chase rumors. She took a shower, which didn't get that smell out of her nose. Her tiny house was an oven, despite the heat pumped she'd wasted the last of her divorce settlement money on, and she actually had to turn on the good old fashioned swamp cooler she couldn't bring herself to get rid of.

Theoretically, the desert cooled at night, but lately the coolness had come without benefit of a breeze. She started with the air-conditioner, which was nearly as old as she was, and by midnight, shut it down, shoved a fan in the window, and hoped for the best.

She couldn't sleep. Worries about herself, about Chase, about the appropriateness of the investigation had her pacing. The mentions Chase had made over dinner about rumors concerning the End of the World had her worried as well.

Hope had once been called the Hope of the West. Founded just after the Civil War by philanthropists and political idealists, Hope was supposed to be a refuge for displaced former slaves as well as immigrants who weren't wanted in larger cities, and even Chinese families, so long as they remained in their own enclave at the edge of town.

The founders of Hope put ads in all the major newspapers, promising land and jobs to people no one else wanted. Hope also promised full equality to blacks and immigrants, although "immigrants" did not include the Chinese, who wouldn't be allowed to vote or hold office. Hope was notable in its Chinese relations, though, for allowing entire families to live there, so long as they kept to themselves. Most states only tolerated Chinese males.

The experiment didn't last. The United States barred Chinese immigration in the early part of the 20th century, and then the State of Oregon itself started enforcing the discrimination built into its constitution, attempting to bodily throw Hope's blacks out of the state. The entire town prevented that, letting the blacks stay so long as the city (and county) promised not to let them hold elected office or take state jobs.

Still, Hope was something of a legend in the state, a place where people could be perceived as nothing more than a set of skills. Where, in the words of Martin Luther King Jr., people could be judged by the content of their character instead of the color of their skin.

That was Hope's legacy, and the reason for its name. Hope's children got spoon-fed this history from the moment they walked into Hope Elementary, and heard about it all the way to graduation from Hope High.

So the idea of a massacre, any massacre, particularly one that someone remembered and tried to hide, went against everything Hope stood for. People didn't die here, not in large groups. Hell, they didn't die in small ones.

Becca got out of bed, grabbed her lightest robe—which Chase had bought her for one of their anniversaries—and headed for the couch, the television, and late-night talk shows. Maybe some blathering would shut down her brain.

Because all this thinking about a possible massacre—even one nearly a hundred years old—upset her more than she wanted to admit.

THEN

They waited until it was full dark before she grew herself back to human. It took a long time.

Jess Taylor's cabin had three rooms and a windowless room he called a storage room. It scared her. It was like the box, only bigger, and it was in the middle of all three rooms—like it took a part off the corners of them and made its own little space.

She had never seen anything like that. He said he kept things in there, but there wasn't much, a few boxes pushed against a corner, and some jars filled with jam.

All three walls had hangers for lanterns. He hung one before he brought her into the room. He kept it on low, so it wouldn't burn too much kerosene and stink up the place—or start a fire. (At least, she hoped it wouldn't start a fire; she'd seen too much fire this day.)

He took the box off the table, talking to her the whole time, mostly nonsense stuff like humans did with babies, stuff about how it would be okay, and the room might be close, but it would do, no one could see in, they would be safe.

She wasn't sure about safe. She wasn't sure about trusting Jess Taylor any more, but she had to. She didn't know what other choice she had.

He set her box on top of the other boxes, then propped the door partly open with one of the jars.

"I'll let you just change now," he said, like she was going to put on a dress. "Let me know when you're done."

"No!" she said, as loud as she could, which wasn't very loud, considering. She didn't have the body behind the sound, and she didn't know she needed it until just now.

That scared her too.

She finally realized how truly helpless she was.

"You have to stay," she said.

He sighed, keeping one hand on the door. "I'm sure it's private. We—folks like me—we let each other be private."

"I got to see you," she said.

"I'll be just outside the door," he said.

"To change," she said. "I got to see you to change. I can't do it without an example."

He frowned. "I can't…change…like you. I can't show you how."

She shook her head. "To look at. I need to see what I'm changing into."

And even then it might not work.

His head bowed, and his arm dropped. "I'm not sure I want to be here for that."

She wasn't sure she could do it without him. In the past, Momma or Daddy had always helped her. They had always found a way to get her through the difficult parts, like making the fingers different lengths or remembering to grow hair.

"How about I stand just outside the door with my back to you?" he asked. "Would that help?"

"Can you tell me if I get it wrong?" she asked.

He bowed his head even more, but he finally said, "I guess I could. Wait one moment, all right?"

She was scared. She knew that just as he left the room. If he hadn't propped open the door, she would've been even more scared. She couldn't see him at all.

Then he came back, carrying a sheet. "I don't have girl clothes. We'll have to find some for you. Can you put this on?"

Modesty, Daddy called it.

Silly, Momma called it, especially when it got really hot. But they learned how to wear things, and taught her about it too.

The clothes she'd been wearing when she was running probably got absorbed into her skin as fuel when she became the sidewalk. She'd been so scared, she hadn't noticed.

She'd most likely be sick later.

"If I put that on, how will you know if I get things right?" she asked.

"I'm sure no one'll notice and you'll do just fine," he said, running the words together like he couldn't breathe.

"I never got everything right before on the first try," she said.

"You'll do fine," he repeated and eased out the door, leaving the sheet on one of the shelves.

It took her a long time to squinch to the edge of the box. By then, she'd formed fingers (probably because she'd been thinking of them) and they were the wrong lengths. But they were good for grabbing onto stuff, especially when she was squinching, so she didn't pay attention to right or wrong.

When she reached the edge of the box, she either had to get all the way to the floor or she had to make legs. She couldn't quite remember the details of legs. The knees she knew and the ankles—they were the bendy parts—and the feet, but there was other stuff she'd forgotten about and she knew they'd look funny.

And she also knew if she hooked the legs up wrong, they'd be impossible to move. So she made hips too.

In fact, everything would be better if she did the bendy parts first. She just finished elbows when Jess Taylor leaned partway in the door, keeping his face averted.

"You all right?"

"Yeah," she said because she didn't know how else to answer.

"Will you be a lot longer?"

"I don't know." She didn't know how long she'd already been. She didn't really care. It took a lot of concentration to make herself all over again, and because she'd been so scared earlier, it was going to be harder.

Just him asking the question knocked her off for a little while. She put one of the elbows just above the hip, and she had to reform, trying to remember exactly how arms bend.

Finally, she had a guess at the human shape she used to wear—just that morning even though it seemed like forever ago—she grabbed the sheet and held it in front of her.

"Is this all right?" she asked.

Jess Taylor turned very slowly. And then he looked at her.

He was trying not to show how he felt, but she could see it in his eyes. Confused, sickened, surprised, all at the same time.

"Close," he said after a minute. "You're really close."

But it took most of the night just to get the general shape right—collarbones, she always forgot about collarbones—and somewhere along the way, he forgot about the sheet, telling her to make a belly button—which she'd never heard of—and explaining dimples in the knees.

By the time they got done, she had a hunch she was more human looking up close than any of her other people had ever been, and the thought made her sad.

But she didn't have long for sad. Because Jess Taylor gave her some bread and some water and an apple that he'd kept in the root cellar since last fall, and told her he needed just a little sleep before going to work.

"You're going to leave me?" she said.

"I have to," he said. "You'll be safe if you don't let anybody see you. They can't know you're here. I'll be back late afternoon. Maybe with some answers."

Maybe. She wanted him to promise her. But he couldn't promise her.

He couldn't promise her anything. Anything at all.

NOW

IF THIS WERE A NORMAL INVESTIGATION regarding a murder that involved the town's history, Becca would go to the Blue Diamond Café. The Blue Diamond was in the exact center of town, in a building that had housed it since the 1930s. Tourists occasionally wandered into the Blue Diamond, saw the ripped booths and dirty windows, and wandered right out.

Becca looked at the Blue Diamond with longing as she walked past. Even though all the city old-timers would be long gone by now—it was the very late hour of 9 a.m.— she'd still find someone to welcome her and give her a free omelet that, in her private moments, she called a heart attack on a plate.

But she had to go two buildings down, to the Hope Historical Society, housed rent-free in one of Chase's renovations, the Hope Bankers Building and Trust.

The money people had long moved away from the Bankers Building, but they'd left behind one of the most solid brick buildings in all of Eastern Oregon. Chase had turned the lower floor into shops and restaurants, the second and third floors into offices, and the upper three floors into condos that sold for four times what Becca paid for her house just two years ago.

There was a diner in the Bankers Building, a 1950s wannabe called the Rock and Remember, and it was usually crammed with transplanted Californians or tourists or both. But the omelets, while large here, were made with egg-whites only, and the chefs—if you could call them that—used only "the good oils"—no butter or lard—which gave the food a cardboard aftertaste. Even the coffee wasn't coffee: it was a mochaccino or a cappuccino or an espresso, something that required a language all its own to order.

Still, she went inside, grabbed a double-tall latte with sprinkles and a "cuppa plain Joe," and then went to the elevator.

The only way she could get Gladys Conyers to talk to her, after that last disastrous interview, was to ply her with her favorite beverage, while making the bribe seem entirely accidental.

Gladys Conyers was forty-five and earnest, a California transplant herself who desperately wanted to convince the entire town of Hope that she was a local. She had some claim. Her grandparents were born here, her parents were raised here, and she spent every summer here from the day she was born.

Her grandfather, Jack Conyers, started the Hope Historical Society as a labor of love in the 1950s, after he came back from the war. He thought every small American town should have its history engraved on its downtown so Americans knew what a wonderful place they came from.

In addition to keeping all of Hope's newspapers, as well as any clippings that pertained to the city from any other periodical—even the flashy *New York Times* article forty years ago that put Hope's ski resorts on the map—, he also managed to acquire important items from Hope's history.

He used to run a small museum from the back of the Historical Society, but lately, he'd been involved in a fund-raising drive to give Hope its own historical museum.

Becca knew she wouldn't find Jack at the Historical Society. He had become understandably hard to reach these last few years, ever since his eighty-fifth birthday. He figured he only had a good ten years left, and he wanted to spend them preserving Hope's history, not talking to people who had questions they could easily answer on their own.

So Gladys had taken over the society. She had a lot of knowledge about Hope—more than most long-time residents, but nothing like her grandfather. Still, anyone who wanted to see Jack had to go through Gladys. If she could answer the questions, then she would and Jack wouldn't lose precious time talking about the past he supposedly loved.

The society had an office on the first floor because it sold items from various ski tournaments and rodeos as well as Hope memorabilia.

Becca tried to ignore the memorabilia, just as she tried to ignore the weird milky scent of the latte she carried in its cardboard holder. She headed to the back, past the teenager manning the sales desk, to the office where Gladys held court.

"Don't think a latte's gonna get me to do you any favors," Gladys said from behind the slatted door. The woman had to have a nose like a Great Dane.

Becca pushed the door open, set the latte on Gladys's specially made cup holder in the center of her desk, then grabbed her own cuppa plain Joe and sat in the easy chair.

"I'm not asking for a favor," Becca said.

"I hear you stopped the work at the Natatorium," Gladys was slender, tanned, and overdressed for Hope. She wore a designer suit—pastel, of course, since it was summer—sandal pumps, and too much makeup. "We have pictures down at the museum of the Nat being built, being used, and being abandoned. I have a computer list already prepared for you, not that I think it'll do any good."

"Why'd you think I'd be here?" Becca asked.

"You always come here, even when you have a current case. Besides, there's so much opposition to Chase's project, I figured you'd want to know if there's any historical reason for it."

Becca hid her smile behind her paper coffee cup. Gladys would be useful after all.

"Is there any historical reason?" Becca asked.

Gladys made a pfumph sound that she had to have learned from her curmudgeonly grandfather. "Besides the rumors of ghosts, of hauntings, of strange sounds in the night?"

"I know about those," Becca said.

"Wow," Gladys said, peeling the lid off her latte and adding even more sugar, "you actually admit you know something."

Becca sighed, and bit back her response. She knew she'd be in for some of this. Twice she had bypassed Gladys and gone to Jack directly, and neither of them let her forget it. For nearly a year, she had to send another officer to ask historical questions. Just recently, Becca had heard through the grapevine that she was welcome at the Historical Society again, so long as she respected its director.

She did respect its director, but she respected its director's grandfather more. Jack could answer her questions quickly and with a minimum of fuss. Gladys had to be babied, which Becca proceeded to do.

"I'm sorry about that," Becca said.

Gladys waved a beringed right hand. "Water under the bridge."

They continued that game until Gladys finished sugaring her latte and put the lid back on. Then she took a sip, eyed Becca, and said, "I hear there are some serious problems at the site."

Becca nodded. One more game, but a quick one. "You know I can't talk about the details, but there is a case."

"Murder?" Gladys asked.

"Sure looks that way," Becca said.

Gladys's eyes glinted. She loved crime and punishment so long as it didn't involve her family.

"Right now, I'm waiting for the crime lab," Becca said, "and while I'm stalled, I thought I'd ask you about a few other things I saw at the Nat."

Gladys tapped the lid of her latte. "Chase already had us run the history of the place. Aside from the usual drownings and accidental deaths that any long-running sports facility would have, we found nothing."

Becca nodded. She would take this one slow. "What about the ghost rumors?"

"Those are mostly from the hotel," Gladys said. "Apparently quite a few shady characters stayed there, as well as some famous folk. President Coolidge was the most famous, I would say. He loved the fishing up here. There are rumors that Hoover stayed there too, but I haven't been able to track them down. People weren't so proud of him, by the end."

Becca didn't need that kind of history lesson. "I'm more concerned with the Nat. Do you know what kind of laborers built it?"

"Of course I do." Gladys opened a drawer in her desk and pulled out a thick file. In it were computer reprints of the society's photos, articles on the construction of the End of the World, and the list that Gladys had mentioned right up front.

She put a lacquered nail on top of one of the photographs. A group of men stood on an empty patch of desert. Some leaned on shovels. Others held pickaxes. A few had rifles.

"These are the men who built the Nat," Gladys said. "We found all sorts of historical photographs for Chase. He loves the authenticity."

Gladys lingered over Chase's name. She'd had a crush on him for years, which bothered Chase a lot more than it bothered Becca.

"What're the rifles for?" Becca asked.

"Chase asked the same thing." Gladys spun the photograph so that she could look at it before spinning it back to Becca. "My grandfather says that the End of the World was so far out of town that the workers brought their guns, hoping that that night's dinner would lope past while they were working. This was jack rabbit country, back in the day, and from what I hear, you could find—and shoot—a rabbit as easily as a fly. The men got their paycheck and that night's supper."

"Was there labor trouble then?"

"In the 20s? In Oregon?" Gladys raised her voice just enough so that the teenager manning the sales desk could hear how stupid Becca was. "I'm sure in Portland, but not in Hope. And the End of the World was built around 1910, not the 20s. It became the premiere resort in this part of the country by 1918, with war vets bringing their brides here for a honeymoon. And I hear rumors that there was quite a speakeasy run out of the hotel's basement. The owners stocked up when it became clear that the dries were going to win."

Becca set the idea of the speakeasy aside for the moment. "What about among the crew? Troubles? Firings?"

"Do they look troubled?" Gladys tapped that nail on the photo again. "Take a close look. What do you see?"

Becca repressed a sigh and leaned forward. Gladys always made these visits seem like an oral exam. "A group of very rough-looking men."

"Well, they'd take any of our modern men and pound them into the ground, that's for sure," Gladys said, a trace of the Valley Girl she'd pretended to be still lingering in her speech. "But I mean their racial mix. Several black men standing side-by-side with several whites. Not even the Chinese are segregated in this photograph, and usually the old photographs kept all the minorities separate—or even more common, out of the picture altogether."

Becca peered at it. The men were touching shoulders, which wasn't something a racially mixed group did in those days.

"There are a few Native Americans as well," Gladys said. "I learned that from their names. These men are so grimy, it's hard to tell much else."

Becca nodded, then frowned. "So the building of the Nat went smoothly, then."

"And the building of the hotel. The rumors about the End of the World started after it opened for business," Gladys said.

"You mean the haunting."

"And the bad dreams. Those were the worst. People would stay at the End of the World, and wake up screaming. The interesting thing is that they all had the same complaint."

Becca swirled the coffee in her cup. She'd have to listen to this even though it wasn't what she had asked. She didn't care about the hauntings. All old hotels had ghost stories. She wanted to hear about the Nat.

"Which was?"

"That they'd had nightmares, and in the nightmares, they saw their long-dead relatives, begging for help." Gladys added a spooky tone to her voice, as if she actually believed this nonsense.

"Wow," Becca said, trying not to sound sarcastic. "Scary."

"No kidding. I've never heard of this kind of haunting."

"But nothing from the Nat?"

"Why do you ask? What did you find?"

"Evidence that something awful happened there as the place was being built," Becca said.

"What kind of awful?" Gladys asked.

"I was hoping you could tell me."

Gladys frowned at her, and Becca had to hide a smile again. For once Gladys had to be feeling as if she were taking a quiz.

"I've never heard a thing, and you'd think in this town, I would." She slid the picture back and studied it as if it held the answers. Then she put it in the file, and closed it.

For a moment, Becca thought the interview was over, and then Gladys said, "Here's what I know. I know the Natatorium was initially supposed to be an indoor tennis court which was, in its day, a revolutionary idea. That was about 1905 or so, when tennis was very popular, particularly out west."

"You're kidding," Becca said.

Gladys actually smiled at her. "Think of all those photographs of women in their long gowns, holding tennis rackets. These women played, and some played very well, despite the handicap."

Becca shook her head. "I thought it was an East Coast thing."

"Every small western town had courts, if they had respectable women. Most of the women were barred from the saloons and the clubs, so they had to have something to do or they might form a temperance society, or a ladies aide society or do something to take away the men's fun."

"Aren't we always that way?" Becca asked, and smiled.

Gladys smiled back. "It didn't work. They didn't build the tennis court for some reason, I never could find out why. The pool came later. It used the tennis court's foundation as the part of the pool itself, and then got built from there."

"Isn't that unusual?" Becca asked.

Gladys shrugged. "Construction in those days was haphazard. I don't know what was usual and what wasn't. I mean, a place could be as sturdy as the hotel or it could be some boards knocked together to be called a house. Really, though, they were just shanties."

"I thought Hope didn't have a shanty town."

"Oh, we did, but it burned," Gladys said. "No one bothered to rebuild it. Folks didn't like to talk about that day. The entire city could've gone up in flames. Somehow it didn't happen, though."

This was one of the things Becca hated about seeing either Conyers about Hope history—their tendency to digress.

"But nothing else about the Nat? Nothing unusual?"

"No, not even the Nat was unusual. They had Natatoriums all over Oregon. They started as playgrounds for the rich—mostly pools and tennis—and then as they fell apart, they became the community pools and playgrounds for the poorer kids. Most of them got shut down in the polio scares of the late 1940s and early 1950s. I think ours is the last one standing, which makes it eligible for historical preservation."

"Which Chase has begged you not to apply for until he's done with the work, right?"

Gladys nodded. "Nothing wrong with that. He doesn't want the extra inspectors. He does the work better than the national preservation standards ask for, so we have no objections here."

"We" being Gladys and her grandfather.

"I hesitate to ask this," Becca said, mostly because she was afraid of Gladys's reaction, "but could you ask your grandfather about the Nat? It's important."

"I'm sure he doesn't know more than I do. It predates him, you know."

"I know," Becca said. "I'm not looking for the official history. I'm looking for rumors or strange comments or stories that he gives no credence to."

"Grandfather ignores anything that can't be proven," Gladys said with something like pride. "If you want innuendo, go see Abigail Browning. She knows every old story about Hope—and most of them are just plain lies."

Becca had forgotten about Abigail Browning. She had been Jack Conyers' assistant—and first major resource—until they had some sort of falling out in the 1950s. For a while, she tried to run the "real" Hope Historical Society, but no one would give her funding, which she said was because she was a woman. Jack Conyers always claimed it was because she knew nothing about history.

She had become one of the town's characters until the transplanted Californian who started Hope's weekly "alternative" paper, printed a story about an affair Abigail Browning and Jack Conyers had. The story was supposed to be sympathetic to Abigail—see how poorly this married man treated this sad spinster lady—but it had the opposite effect. Abigail lost any support she had among the locals for trying to steal Jack Conyers from his still-living, still-popular wife.

Becca would talk to Abigail Browning. But Becca also wanted to talk to Jack Conyers.

She stood. "Please do ask him."

"Oh, I will," Gladys said. "But I'm sure he won't know more than I do."

And with that, Becca knew she had no hope of seeing the town's official historian. So she'd see the unofficial one, and hope for the best.

THEN

THE CABIN GOT REALLY HOT that day and she wanted to open a window, but she was scared to. Mostly she slept and she hoped Jess Taylor would come back for her. She had to keep reminding herself that it was his cabin, he'd be back, but he didn't seem to have many things there, and Daddy had run away from more, so maybe Jess Taylor would too.

Finally, Jess Taylor came back, looking tired and even more scared than when he'd left. His shirt was covered with sweat and some dirt ran along the side of his face. He had one of those overcoats—the short ones Daddy called a suit coat—and he hung it on a chair.

She stood beside the table, and waited for him to tell her to leave.

He looked at her, his big eyes sad. "I have bad news."

She held her breath. She wasn't sure what she'd do when he let her out of here. She hadn't eaten anything since that apple, and even though she took some water because she couldn't help herself—it was so hot inside—she would tell him and offer to repay him. Somehow. Maybe then he wouldn't turn her over to those people.

"Your mother," he said—and she let out a bit of that breath—"Your mother and the other people?...they're gone."

Her stomach clenched. "Gone?"

"That's what we say when we mean they died, honey."

Her cheeks heated. Everyone had told her Daddy was gone too.

"I thought it just meant they went away," she said.

"It's a euphemism."

She'd never heard the word.

He shook his head tiredly. "A word we use when we don't want to be blunt. There are a lot of euphemisms in our language."

She nodded, even though she wasn't sure she understood.

"You're sure she's…gone?" She asked.

"Oh, I'm sure," he said, and shuddered. "You wouldn't ask if you knew the day I had today."

"What did you do?" she asked.

"Work white men wouldn't do," he said. "They consider what I did the dirty work."

She frowned. "What did you do?"

"I'm supposed to sit in a bank," he said. "But they said, *If you want to keep your job, you'll*—"

He stopped. Studied her like he wasn't sure what to say. Then sighed.

"I helped bury them, Sarah."

"Bury?" She knew what that was, at least. She'd seen it— the wooden boxes, the holes in the ground, the markers. "If they had the boxes and stuff, how did you know my mother was there?"

It seemed to take him a minute to understand her. Then he nodded, once. "There were no boxes, honey," he said gently. "They were just placed in the ground."

Barbaric, that's what it is, her daddy said. *How can they do that to their own?*

It's a religious custom, her mother said. *We used to have them too.*

"And they were dead?" she asked, her voice small.

"Oh, yeah," he said, and shuddered. "They were dead."

"Where are they?" she asked. "Where did you bury them?"

He studied her for a long time, as if he thought about whether or not to answer her.

Then he sighed again.

"It's a place they call the End of the World."

NOW

ABIGAIL BROWNING LIVED in a fairytale cottage at the end of one of Hope's oldest streets. Large trees, which somehow thrived despite the desert air, surrounded the place, making it look even more like something out of Hansel and Gretel. Blooming plants lined the walk, plants which Becca knew took more water than summer water rationing allowed. She decided to ignore them as she stood on the brick steps and rapped on the solid oak door.

A latch slammed back and then the door pulled open, sending a wave of lavender scent outside. The woman who stood before Becca was short and hunched, not the tall powerhouse that Becca remembered from her childhood.

"Abigail Browning?" Becca asked.

"Don't you recognize me, Rebecca Keller? I practically raised you."

That wasn't quite true. Abigail Browning did baby-sit when Becca's parents couldn't find anyone else, but otherwise she had little to do with Becca's childhood.

"Sure I do, Mrs. Browning," Becca said, falling back on her childhood name for this woman, even though Abigail Browning had never married. "I was wondering if you could help me with a case."

Abigail Browning smiled and stepped away from the door. "Of course, my dear. Would you like some tea?"

"I'd love some," Becca said as she walked inside. The house smelled the same—lavender and baking bread with the faint undertone of cat.

Now Becca was old enough to appreciate the mahogany staircase, built Craftsman-style, and the matching bookcases that graced the living room. The entire house had mahogany trim as well as built-in shelving, a feature Becca knew that Chase would love—particularly since no one had painted over the original wood.

Mrs. Browning led her into the kitchen. A coffee cake sat in a glass case in the center of the table, almost as if Mrs. Browning had expected her. Mrs. Browning filled a kettle and put it on the stove, then climbed on a stool to remove large mugs from the shiny mahogany cupboards.

"I'm not as tall as I used to be," she said. "Time crushes all of us."

Becca nodded, uncertain what to say. "The kitchen looks just the same."

"Which negates the ten thousand dollar remodel I did two years ago," Mrs. Browning said.

Becca looked at her in surprise.

"I had to update everything. I had dry rot. Or the house did. Your husband helped me."

Becca opened her mouth to correct Mrs. Browning, then thought the better of it. Abigail Browning often made misstatements to see how other people stood on things.

"He's a good man," Mrs. Browning said. "Maybe the best in town, and you let him get away."

"I didn't let—"

"You confused him with your father, who was a horrid, manipulative man, and you forgot that men can be strong without being horrid."

Becca felt her cheeks heat. "Would you like to hear about the case?"

"More than you'd like to hear how you threw away a good man because a bad one raised you," Mrs. Browning said, taking down two plates.

Becca did not offer to help her. Instead, Becca stood near the table, hands crossed in front of her, feeling ten years old again.

"So tell me," Mrs. Browning said, putting the plates on the table. The kettle whistled, and she removed it from the heat. She grabbed a tea pot from a shelf that looked old, but had to be new because Becca didn't remember it.

"I was wondering what you know about the Natatorium."

"I can tell you how awful it smelled when I was a child, but that's not what you're asking, is it? Be specific, girl. Didn't I teach you anything?"

"What happened when it was built?"

"Which time?" Mrs. Browning set a beautiful wood trivet on the table, then placed the teapot on top of it.

"Which time?" Becca repeated. "Things are only built once, aren't they?"

Mrs. Browning stood near a chair near the teapot shelf, a chair that Becca remembered had always been Mrs. Browning's favorite. Becca had sat there once as a child, and had found it uncomfortable, molded to the elderly woman's body. Only then Mrs. Browning hadn't been elderly. She had only seemed that way.

"The foundation for the Natatorium was laid at the same time as the hotel, around 1908. It was abandoned that same year."

"Abandoned?" Becca asked. "I heard that the work stopped."

"Probably from that horrible Gladys Conyers. She really knows only the textbook history of this town which, I'm sorry to say, is wrong. People are never saints, you know. You always have to look for the darkness to balance the light."

Mrs. Browning peered at her. Mrs. Browning's eyes, buried under layers of wrinkles, were the same piercing blue they had always been.

Becca remembered Mrs. Browning trying to tell her that before. *You're the light, Rebecca. Remember that. Good things can come from dark places.*

She shook the memory away.

"Sit down, child, you're making me nervous."

Becca slid into her usual chair. Odd to think she had a usual chair, when she hadn't been to this house in more than twenty years.

"Do you still remember how to pour?"

Becca smiled. She did remember those lessons. Mrs. Browning had trained her in "company" manners, including how to set a table, how to dress for dinner, and how to pour for guests.

"I do," Becca said. She picked up the tea pot, handling it as if Mrs. Browning had pulled down her silver service instead of her every day.

Mrs. Browning watched her every move as if she were still being judged on perfection. Becca remembered everything, including when to ask if Mrs. Browning wanted sugar and cream, and to hold the top of the pot so that it wouldn't fall unceremoniously into Mrs. Browning's plate.

Mrs. Browning smiled, as if Becca's behavior was confirmation of the work she'd done bringing her up.

"So," Mrs. Browning said when Becca finished pouring, "which part of the Natatorium are you interested in? The first building or the second?"

"I'm interested in the pool, whenever it was laid."

"The pool." Mrs. Browning pursed her lips. "So your Chase finally found the bodies, did he?"

Becca felt her breath catch. Whatever she'd expected Mrs. Browning to say, it wasn't that.

"You knew?"

"Child, half the town knew. Why do you think that no one was allowed near that old wreck?"

"But you swam there as a child."

"All of us did," Mrs. Browning said. "And some of us brought our own children there, until the place shut down. It was just a rumor, after all. Except for the hotel."

Becca frowned. "We're talking about the Nat."

"We can't talk about the Nat without talking about the hotel. Have you ever been inside?"

"Just last night, as a matter of fact."

"Did you look at the walls?"

Becca's frown grew deeper. "Yes."

"Then you understand why I told your Chase not to tear them down."

"No," Becca said. "I don't."

Mrs. Browning touched her hand with dry fingers. "Rebecca, you've never been slow. Haven't you wondered why those walls move?"

"They don't move," Becca said. "They have heat shimmers. It piles up and—"

"Heat shimmers occur on pavement in sunlight," Mrs. Browning said. "Not in a dark dusty hotel in the middle of a summer evening."

Becca licked her lips. When she was fourteen, she'd run from that hotel. She'd gone there to neck with Zack Wheeler, and when he'd pressed her against one of the walls, it was squishy. She turned to look at the wood, saw it shimmer, change, and shimmer again, and she couldn't help it.

She screamed.

Zack saw it too, grabbed her hand, and pulled her out of there. They'd run all the way to his car, and even told his father, who had looked at them with contempt. That was the first time Becca had heard the heat shimmer idea, but it wasn't the last.

"So what causes it?" Becca asked.

"Aliens," Mrs. Browning said. "The aliens haunting the End of the World."

THEN

SHE COULDN'T GO TO THE END OF THE WORLD. She couldn't even leave the house. Jess Taylor didn't want her to. He was afraid for her. She was hot and sad and lonely, and she spent her days crying sometimes.

But she didn't practice changing. Instead, she worked on getting every detail right. Jess Taylor had to tell her sometimes that she was using masculine details—he'd actually laughed the time she put bits of hair on her own chin—but mostly, he said, she was looking solid.

Whatever that meant.

He wanted the town to think no one had survived. He didn't want them to question her or him.

It took him days and days to figure out how to do that.

Then one day he told her. She was going to take a train.

NOW

ALIENS? OF ALL THE THINGS BECCA had expected from Mrs. Browning, a popular crazy notion wasn't one of them. Hope had been the talk of the alien conspiracy community since 2001, when one of her colleagues had discovered some metal in Lake Waloon. The lake had receded during one of the driest years on record, leaving all sorts of artifacts in its cracked and much-abused bed.

The experts, called in by the Historical Society, claimed it was part of an experimental airplane or maybe even one of the early do-it-yourself models from the 1920s.

UFO groupies looked at the pictures on the internet, and descended *en masse* to Hope, believing they'd found another ship like the one the government supposedly hid in Roswell, New Mexico.

Ever since, Hope had to endure annual pilgrimages from the UFO faithful. Becca tried to ignore them, just like she used to ignore the Deadheads when they came through on their way to Eugene to see the Grateful Dead in its natural habitat.

"Aliens," Becca said. "Surely you don't believe that hype from a few years ago—"

"Yes," Mrs. Browning said as she cut Becca a piece of coffee cake. "Of course I do. I grew up knowing that we'd been invaded. The fact that the ship was found simply confirmed it."

"The ship wasn't found," Becca said, and then caught herself. She'd learned in a few short months not to argue with the True Believers. Only she'd never taken Mrs. Browning to be one of them.

Mrs. Browning cut another piece of coffee cake and slid it onto her own plate. "If you do not believe that twisted hunk of metal was an alien spacecraft, then you won't believe anything I have to tell you about the Natatorium."

Becca sighed. "I saw the so-called ship. It's just a crumpled aircraft."

"No," Mrs. Browning said. "It was molded to look like an aircraft. It's a space ship."

Becca had heard this argument countless times as well. She took a deep breath, and then thought the better of all of it.

"All right," she said. "Let's pretend that you and I agree. Let's pretend that is a spaceship, and the squirming wall in the End of the World is made by alien ghosts. What else can you tell me?"

Mrs. Browning delicately cut her piece of coffee cake with her fork, her little finger extended. She had the same manners she always had. She seemed as sharp as she had thirty years ago.

But Becca knew that sometimes elderly people who lived alone developed "peculiarities." Now she was going to have to overlook Mrs. Browning's just to get to the heart of the story.

And maybe, just maybe, she was going to have to accept that she was wasting her time.

"Eat," Mrs. Browning said, "and I'll tell you what I know."

THEN

SHE HADN'T BEEN THAT FRIGHTENED since Jess Taylor found her. She thought he was going to make her leave by train.

She didn't know where he'd send her or what she'd do or who she'd meet. But by now, she knew she could trust him. He brought her clothes. He fed her. He helped her.

They had long talks when he got home from the bank, and one night, he told her his family had died just like hers.

"In Hope?" she asked.

He shook his head. "Far away from Hope in a place called Mississippi."

"How come you didn't get killed?" she asked. She already knew he couldn't change, so she wanted to know how he got away.

"I was in the North," he said. "Ohio. Going to school in Antioch. Then the money stopped—my whole family was supporting me, giving me an education, and I sent letters to find out why, and someone sent me a postcard back. It was a drawing of the day—of the killings—like people were proud of it, and they said *Don't bother to come*, but I did anyway and…"

His voice trailed away. He didn't look at her. He was quiet a long time.

"What happened?" she asked because she couldn't take it anymore.

"I ran, and ended up in Hope."

NOW

BECCA TOOK A BITE OF HER COFFEE CAKE. It was as good and rich as ever, a taste of her childhood.

Mrs. Browning watched her eat that bite, then leaned back in her own chair. Becca wondered if that position was even comfortable, given Mrs. Browning's pronounced dowager's hump.

"In the summer of Aught Eight, the shanty town just outside of Hope burned to the ground," Mrs. Browning began in her teacherly voice. "Most of the histories do not mention the shanty town. Those that do claim the fire threatened Hope itself. It didn't threaten the buildings that comprised Hope. It threatened the vision of Hope."

Very dramatic, Becca thought.

She took another bite of cake, then followed it with a sip of tea, straining to keep her expression interested and credulous.

"The fire was as controlled a burn as the people of Hope could manage in those bygone days."

The ease with which Mrs. Browning told this story made Becca believe that Mrs. Browning used to recite it as part of the history project.

"The townspeople had gotten together and decided to rid themselves of the strangers once and for all."

Mrs. Browning shook her fork—still holding coffee cake—at Becca.

"If you look in the papers of the time, you'll see references to the strangers. They arrived in 1900, claiming to have lost their wagon several miles back. They had no luggage, few belongings, and they spoke a strange version of English. The locals thought they were ignorant immigrants who'd been tricked by their guide, and gave them some land just outside of town."

"Where the End of the World is?" Becca asked.

Mrs. Browning raised her eyebrows. "Am I telling this or are you?"

"Sorry," Becca said.

"Where that 1970s mall is. It's now near the center of town. But then, it was just outside, on land no one wanted. The strangers built their own little cabins—poorly. They looked like they didn't know what to do, and of course, no one was going to help them much more than provide a meal or some supplies. They got a bit of work too."

Becca nodded, wishing Mrs. Browning would get on with it.

"I don't know what happened. The reference in various letters I've seen is that the strangers confirmed their demonic qualities. I have no idea what that means or how they confirmed demonic qualities, but the upshot is that the town fathers asked them to leave. The strangers said they wouldn't. The fight went on for some months, when finally the shanty town burned."

"A controlled burn," Becca said. "Started by?"

"Anyone who's everyone," Mrs. Browning said. "I never asked. Besides, everyone would've told me they had nothing to do with it. But you'll notice—well, of course you won't, they're all dead—but I noticed when I was young just how many of the older generation carried some burn marks on their hands. Except for that controlled burn, and the loss of a building here and there, Hope was one of the few western communities that didn't have a serious fire. And not all of these men worked for the Hope Volunteer Fire Department."

Becca finished her coffee cake. Then she picked up her tea mug and cradled it. "So they burned the shanty town. What has that to do with the Natatorium?"

"It was being built. The hotel was just a shell—it wasn't nearly done yet—and the Nat was dug, but not poured. It was going to be a tennis court. In those days, I believe the courts were clay. Not that it matters. It never got finished."

"Because…?" Becca was trying to keep the frustration from her voice.

"Because the town hated the place. It reminded them that they hadn't lived up to that promise we all learned about."

Becca gripped the mug tightly. "I still don't see the connection."

Mrs. Browning sighed, as if Becca were a particularly slow student. "They used the fire to round up the strangers and herd them to the Nat. Do I need to spell it out for you?"

"You're saying the town killed these strangers?" Becca asked. "And buried them under the Nat?"

"Yes." Mrs. Browning sounded exasperated.

"How many?"

"I don't know. No one kept records. I heard that they tried to bury them under the hotel, and when that didn't work, they went to the Nat. That's why the ghosts haunt the hotel."

"You'd think they'd haunt the Nat," Becca said.

"Hauntings aren't logical," Mrs. Browning said.

None of this was, Becca thought. "How do you know that these strangers were aliens, not just a group of Eastern Europeans who ran into some people who didn't understand them?"

"Because of the stories," Mrs. Browning said. "They had glowing eyes. They talked gibberish. They could seem taller than they were. And they came from nowhere. There were no wagon tracks. There was no wagon. And these people had no idea how people behaved. Not how Americans behaved, but how human beings behaved. They had to learn it all."

Becca shook her head. "I'm sorry, Mrs. Browning. But humans differ greatly. And if this group had been from a very different culture, the residents of Hope could have made the same charge. Aliens is as farfetched as it came."

Mrs. Browning smiled sadly. "I believe it was aliens."

"Why?" Becca asked.

"Because I met one," Mrs. Browning said.

THEN

THE TRAIN WAS BIG AND DIRTY AND SMELLY. Ash fell everywhere. It made an awful noise and she wanted to run away from it.

Jess Taylor stood beside her, holding her hand. He'd borrowed his neighbor's wagon, and they'd come to the small town of Brothers, which was two stops away from Hope.

"Remember," he said. "Tomorrow, you come here, and give the nice man this paper, and then you get on the train going that direction."

He pointed. He'd already shown her the engine, and how you could tell what direction a train was going in.

"I'll meet you at the station, and we'll pretend that we haven't seen each other in years. Okay?"

He'd told her all this before, and then it sounded easy, but now, it just sounded terrifying. She wanted to get back in the wagon, get back in his house, and hide there forever.

But he said, now that her people were gone, she needed to have a life.

Where will I have this life? She asked him.

In Hope, he said. *With me.*

Momma and Daddy said humans didn't do these things, they didn't make that kind of commitment, they didn't understand permanence and obligation and re-sponsibility, which made them dangerous.

But Jess Taylor wasn't dangerous. And he seemed to understand all those words. He seemed to live them.

Only they came back now that she was standing on the platform with him, staring at the train.

"It's only one night," he said. "I already paid for the room. You'll be safe."

She wanted to believe him. But she was scared. What if she changed by accident? What if she said something wrong? Would they make her scream? Would they bury her without a box?

Who would tell Jess Taylor?

How would he ever know?

NOW

"I was just a little girl," Mrs. Browning said, "and she was very old. Older than anyone I'd ever seen. She came to the Natatorium when I was swimming there. She cried."

"She cried?" Becca asked.

Mrs. Browning nodded. "She stood back from the pool, and she cried as she looked at it. My mother was there with me, and she just stared. Then she told me to get my towel. It was time to go."

"I don't understand," Becca said. "How do you know the old woman was an alien."

"There'd always been stories about her," Mrs. Browning said. "She came to town to see her uncle, and she never left. At least that was the story, and some people claimed they saw her get off the train. But a few said the luggage she carried was her uncle's, and that he'd brought her there that very afternoon."

"So?" Becca asked.

"So that was right after the massacre. It was strange that he had a niece no one had ever heard of."

Becca shrugged. "I'm so sorry to be skeptical, Mrs. Browning, but I still don't understand how that translates to alien."

"I saw her once, all by myself. She was sitting at a bus stop near the old bank, and she put her hand on the bench. Her hand slid right through it."

Becca sighed. "You're not going to convince me. Not without some kind of real proof."

"What about those bodies, young lady?" Mrs. Browning said, bringing herself up as close to her old height as she could. "Are those good enough for you? They're not human, are they?"

Becca flashed on the broken femurs, so recognizable. "Of course they are."

Mrs. Browning's cheeks flushed. "You're just saying that."

"Actually," Becca said. "I'm not."

THEN

THAT NIGHT, SHE SLEPT ON A SINGLE BED behind the kitchen of Mrs. Mother's Brothers Boarding House. Colored people—which was her and Jess Taylor, apparently—didn't get their own rooms. They couldn't even really stay at the boarding house, but Jess Taylor knew the cook, who volunteered to share her room. Mrs. Mother, the old lady who ran the place, had frowned in that mean way some humans had, but all she said was, "Make sure it doesn't get into the food."

She didn't understand for the longest time that the "it" Mrs. Mother referred to was her.

Maybe that's why Daddy said this was a dangerous place, why humans were scary people. She hadn't even known they cared about differences, and now she was finding out that the differences were everything.

No wonder they'd gone after her people. She hadn't noticed Jess Taylor's differences from the men at the bank and as time went on, she began to understand how badly her own people had mimicked the humans. No knee dimples, too smooth skin, eyes that didn't blink.

If the dark skin or the long braid of hair running down the back or the upswept eye angle scared them, they must've been really terrified by a whole group of people whose skin had no wrinkles, whose ankles didn't stick out, and whose expressions never changed.

No wonder.

Then she remembered Jess Taylor: *I can't believe I'm defending them* and she knew just how he felt.

The bed in the kitchen had bugs. They bit her during the night. Upstairs people laughed, and the place smelled like grease, and she wanted some water, just so she could wash the bugs off, but she didn't.

She picked them off and squished them between her fingers, and finally she got out of that bed and sat in a rocking chair, and watched out the window until the sun came up.

Then she picked up her little bag, and walked to the train station, just like Jess Taylor had told her to do, and she sat on the far edge of the platform so no one but the man who worked there saw her, and she waited for the train.

NOW

BECCA WAS HAPPY TO LEAVE. Mrs. Browning did tell her other stories about the Natatorium—stories about its first few days as a recreation center, stories about the celebrities who used it—but both Becca and Mrs. Browning knew that the stories were merely Mrs. Browning's way of saving face.

As Becca made her good-byes, holding a piece of that delicious coffee cake in a napkin, both she and Mrs. Browning knew that she would never really trust Mrs. Browning again.

All the way to her car, Becca tried not to let sadness overwhelm her. She had lost more than a source for Hope's history. She'd lost an icon of her youth.

She had always believed that Abigail Browning was a woman of unassailable intellect and integrity. Even through the Conyers' scandal, Becca's opinion did not change. She still nodded at Abigail Browning on the street when others hadn't, and she still revered the woman she had once known.

If anything, the scandal had clarified something for her: Becca finally understood why Mrs. Browning, who had always seemed more knowledgeable than Mr. Conyers, had stopped working at the Hope Historical Society.

Now Becca wasn't so sure. Now she wondered if Mrs. Browning was fired because she believed the strange stories—the ones that had always been part of Hope. Stories of ghosts and aliens and things that went bump in the night.

Becca got into the squad and turned the ignition. The crappy air conditioning felt worse than the heat in Mrs. Browning's garden. Maybe if Becca believed in fairy tales, she would actually believe that Mrs. Browning had some sort of magic that kept the heat and the desert at bay.

But Becca only believed in reality. And only the reality she could see, Chase used to say. She could never envision his projects, not even when she looked at the architectural renderings.

She always had to wait until he was done to understand how perfect his vision had been.

What had Mrs. Browning said about Chase? *You confused him with your father, who was a horrid, manipulative man, and you forgot that men can be strong without being horrid.*

That's what Becca should have asked about. She should have asked what Mrs. Browning meant by that statement—not about Chase: women who hadn't married Chase loved him. (Hell, *Becca* still loved him)—but about her father.

Tell me about your father, her therapist said once.

He was a good man, Becca said.

But he didn't like your job.

Becca had smiled. *He was old-fashioned. He believed women didn't belong outside the home.*

What about in a police car?

Becca had laughed. *Are you kidding? He stopped paying for my school when he heard what I wanted to do.*

Is Chase like him?

Of course not, Becca said.

But your father's action sounds manipulative. You say Chase is manipulative.

Not like that, Becca said. *He respects women.*

Does he respect you?

Becca sighed and leaned back against the seat of the squad. Did he respect her? Yesterday, she would have said no, and she would have said that his secretive call about the Nat proved it.

But couldn't it also be viewed the other way? Couldn't his call be a sign of trust, of faith in her abilities instead of faith in his own ability to control her?

Could Mrs. Browning be right?

Becca shook her head. A headache was forming between her eyes. She put the squad in gear just as her cell rang.

She unhooked it from her belt and looked at the display. Jillian Mills. Becca took the call.

"Can you come down here?" Jillian asked.

"Is this about the Nat?" Becca asked.

"Yeah," Jillian said. "I have the weirdest results."

THEN

THEY TOOK HER TICKET just like Jess Taylor said they would, but they wouldn't let her sit in a chair like everybody else. They put her on one of the platforms in the back. The ash and the dirt and the stink were awful there, and as the train started to pull away, she could see the rails move.

She tried the door to get inside, but someone had locked it. She pounded on it, and the men in the nearby chairs—the men with white skin—laughed at her and pointed and she moved away from the blackened window so that they couldn't see her any more.

She was afraid they'd come out and hurt her.

Like they hurt her Momma.

Like they hurt Jess Taylor's family.

She was scared now, and she tried not to let that change her. Because if she changed, she'd lose this chance. She'd spend her life—what was left of it—as a railing or a board or a door knob. And then, because she couldn't sleep-change, she'd starve and fall off, all decayed, and they'd toss her aside—*what is that dried up thing?*—and she'd die, probably in the nearby sagebrush, all alone.

Just like her Daddy.

The whole trip, she stared straight ahead and clung to her bag and thought about Jess Taylor waiting for her. Thought about shoulders and backs and legs and human forms so that the spikes wouldn't come out of her spine or her eyes wouldn't shift to a different part of her head.

She thought and thought and was surprised when she realized she could hardly wait to get back to Hope.

NOW

BECCA'S STOMACH CLENCHED the entire way to the coroner's office. She wished she hadn't eaten that coffee cake now. She wished she hadn't gone to Mrs. Browning's. She didn't want the thoughts that were crowding her brain. She didn't want to think the weird results were because some aliens were massacred in Hope.

And yet she was thinking just that.

The coroner's office was on a side street behind Hope's main police station. The office wasn't an office at all, more like a science lab, morgue, and training area rolled into one.

The college student who ran the front desk in exchange for rent in the studio apartment above was reading Dostoevsky. He barely looked up as Becca entered.

"She's expecting you," he said.

Becca nodded and continued to the small room that served as Jillian's office. The smell of decay and formaldehyde seemed less here than it did near the door, and wasn't nearly as strong as it was in the basement where the autopsies actually took place.

Jillian was standing behind her desk, sorting paper files. She wore a clean white smock over her clothes—a sure sign that she had just finished an autopsy—and had her hair pulled back with a copper barrette.

"Your life just got easier," Jillian said without preamble.

"How's that?" Becca asked.

"Close the door."

Becca did.

"I did some preliminary work before calling the state crime lab," Jillian said. "Those bodies down there, they're not human."

Becca felt a shiver run down her back.

"I'm not sure what they are. I'm not even sure they are bodies."

Becca gripped the back of the nearest chair. She didn't want Mrs. Browning to be right.

"What are they then? Aliens?"

Jillian laughed. "Of course not. Whatever gave you that idea?"

"Abigail Browning," Becca said.

"Oh, our local UFOlogist," Jillian said. "You know she's been making her living these last few years providing historical tours of Lake Waloon?"

How could Becca have missed that? So Abigail Browning had a stake in keeping the alien story alive. And what could be better than a tale of alien massacre?

Hell, that would even give her a measure of revenge against Jack Conyers, showing that the story of racial unity in Hope was really just a myth.

"Just wondering," Becca said, trying to make light of it.

"Well, we all are. From what I can tell, these are very old bones—if they are bones as we know them. The material is something else, and it's hollow."

"But they looked human."

"So do a lot of things. Mammalian bones tend to look alike. I've had new trainees mistake cat spines and rib-cages for human babies."

Becca swallowed. "What about the smell?"

"Well, that's the odd part," Jillian said. "It's coming from the—whatever they are—bones."

"Huh?"

Jillian shrugged. "Let me show you."

She grabbed an evidence bag from a table beside her desk. Inside was what looked to Becca to be an adult human rib bone. It even had the proper curvature.

"Break it," Jillian said.

"Isn't this destroying evidence?"

"Of what? Alien massacre? Just break it."

Becca grabbed a pair of medical gloves from the box beside Jillian's desk, then opened the evidence bag. She took out the rib bone, and immediately felt a sense of wrongness. It was too squishy. Even bones that had been in damp ground for a long period of time never felt like this—almost like a rubber chew toy that had been well loved.

Becca turned it over in her fingers, feeling a gag reflex, and swallowing hard against it.

Jillian nodded. "Kinda gross, huh?"

Becca didn't answer. Instead, she grabbed both ends of the bone and bent.

If it had been made of rubber—even old rubber—the bone should've bent with her hands. But it didn't bend. It snapped, and a waft of rot filled Becca's nose, almost as if she had put her face in the middle of a decaying corpse.

"Jesus Christ," she said, dropping both pieces into the evidence bag. "You could've warned me."

The gag reflex had gotten worse. Her eyes watered and she resisted the urge to wipe at them. She'd learned that lesson long ago, when she'd been a rookie: *Don't touch your own skin after touching a corpse.*

But that wasn't a corpse. It wasn't even a real bone, at least not of a kind she was familiar with.

"C'mon." Jillian took the sealed evidence bag from her, and led Becca to the back room where cleaning solutions and the sharp-scented nostril-clearing substance that Jillian preferred waited.

Becca inhaled the substance, feeling her nose clear as if she'd sniffed smelling salts, and then she grabbed a clean washcloth, wiped her face, and leaned against a metal filing cabinet.

"So what the hell is it?" she asked.

"I wish I knew. I'm going to be calling not just the state, but some anthropologists to see if they've seen anything like it."

"Then why did you tell me my job got easier?"

"Because," Jillian said. "There's no recent body. There aren't even old bodies. There's a mystery, yes, but it's an archeological one. There's probably some plant or root or something that does this, and maybe it's extinct or something, which is why we're not familiar with it."

"You mean like that death plant?" Becca asked.

"The corpse flower?" Jillian nodded. "I forgot about that. I'll look it up on line. Maybe it used to grow around here."

Becca's fingers tingled. The bone—or whatever it was—had felt alive, but the way that plant roots did. She could believe that Chase had discovered the remains of a very old plant much easier than believing that an alien massacre happened in Hope.

"You want to tell Chase?" Jillian asked. "Or should I?"

Becca felt her breath catch. Chase's dream project was still on. It would still happen.

One day, the End of the World would become the premiere resort in Eastern Oregon.

"He's not going to be able to work for a while. If they think this thing is unusual, they'll do some excavation," Jillian said. "But it's not like a major dig, and it's not a crime scene. He should be thrilled."

Becca smiled in spite of her stinging nose. "Thrilled probably isn't the word I'd use. But he'll be relieved, once he's past the immediate inconvenience."

Jillian crossed her arms, looking amused. "So am I telling him?"

"No," Becca said. "I will."

THEN

The train passed it.

Jess Taylor hadn't warned her.

But there was a big hand-carved sign saying, *Future Home of the End of the World Resort*. And there was a finished building right at the edge, with the word *Hotel* on it. And a big brown patch where somebody had dug a hole and then covered it up.

Her mommy was in there.

She went to the edge of the platform and stared at it until it got tiny in the distance.

And then she remembered: Her daddy, days before he left, telling Momma—

If anything happens, we go to the End of the World. We burrow into the walls or slide against the frames. We become other. We hibernate until our own people return.

She never learned how. Grown ones could do it. And they could coax their children into it, but no child could do it on her own.

She'd only seen the shimmers a few times, back when she was really little, in the ship before it crashed. Lots and lots of her people, people she didn't see until Daddy woke them, shimmered in the back compartment.

Sometimes they'd have dreams and you'd see their ghostly selves, wandering through the ship. She got scared by that, but Momma said it was normal. It was a way to check how time was passing, and when it was safe to wake up.

She didn't see any shimmers as she passed the End of the World.

She didn't see any one she knew. It was quiet and empty and lonely.

Her people were really and truly gone, and now she was the only one left to wait for the others. The ones who were supposed to rescue them.

If they ever came.

NOW

BECCA AND CHASE STOOD at the End of the World, staring at the hole dug into the floor of the Natatorium. It was early evening, little more than twenty-four hours since Chase called Becca to the scene.

The area was quiet—as quiet as the desert got. A high-pitched whine that came from a bug Becca could not identify came from just outside the broken wall. The wind rustled a tarp that covered some of the wood Chase had bought, and not too far away, a bird peeped, probably as it hunted the whining bugs.

The sounds of workers waiting for instructions, the low buzz-growl of her radio unit, the crunch of vans on gravel were in the recent past. Right now, it was just her, Chase, and the plant-like bone-like things half buried in the ground.

The smell wasn't as bad as it had been the day before. The bone-like things weren't freshly broken. The scent was fading, just like the smell of a dead body faded to an annoyance when the body was removed from the scene.

She and Chase stood side-by-side in the patch of sunlight that filtered through the hole in the Natatorium wall. She had brought him down here to tell him the news, and when she finished, he didn't say a word.

He swallowed once, stared at the ground, and then closed his eyes. His entire body trembled. She thought he was going to cry.

Then he took a deep breath, pushed his hardhat back, and frowned. "No one died."

"That's right," Becca said.

"And these aren't bodies."

Not human ones anyway, she almost said, but then felt the joke was in poor taste. For all she knew, Chase could have talked to Mrs. Browning too. He might have heard the alien rumors as well.

"Jillian thinks they're the remains of plants."

"*Thinks?*" Chase asked.

Becca shrugged. "All she knows is that they're not bone, not from humans or from animals. And they're the source of the smell."

"Weird," Chase said.

"You won't be able to work in the Nat for a while," Becca said. "People are coming from U of O and OSU's science and archeological departments to see what they can learn. Jillian thinks they might contact the Smithsonian or someplace like that. She made a ballpark estimate of eight months, but it could be more than that. It could be less."

Chase nodded. He still wasn't looking at her. "I can finish the hotel, though."

"The hotel, the golf course, the houses, you can do all of it.'"

"Golf courses," he reminded her.

"Golf courses," she said.

They stood in silence for a moment longer. Chase had his head bowed, as if he were looking at a grave.

Then he asked, "They'll clear this away?"

"Probably," Becca said. "Or you might have to find a way to build over it. You certainly don't want one of those things to break while guests are using the pool."

He shuddered, then nodded. He took off his hardhat and twisted it between his hands.

"Mrs. Browning says you're keeping the walls of the hotel," Becca said.

He looked at her sideways. "You spoke to Abigail?"

Becca nodded. "You know she used to baby-sit me, way back when."

"That's what she said. She also said I should give you time."

Becca felt her cheeks flush. That old woman meddled. "For what?"

He shrugged and looked away. "I still love you, Becca."

She wondered if that was manipulation. Or if it was just truth. Had she always mistaken truth for manipulation, and manipulation for truth?

Had she thrown away the most important thing in her life because she hadn't recognized it, because she hadn't been prepared for it, because nothing in her life taught her how to understand it?

She had had set ideas on the way that men were, on the ways they treated their wives, on the way they lived their lives.

We all have prejudices, her therapist had once told her, early in their sessions. *The key is recognizing them, and going around them. Because if we don't, we never see what's in front of us.*

Becca looked at the plant-like things. She had initially seen bone because of the smell, but they weren't bone. They just looked like bone. They were harmless and old and a curiosity, but not evidence of a horrible past.

She had misunderstood. Chase had misunderstood. And the End of the World had nearly died once again.

"You really love this place, don't you?" she said to Chase.

"It's the first place I recognized Hope's potential," he said. "It just took me fifteen years to get enough money and clout to bring my dream to reality."

"And this almost ruined it. What would you have done if Mrs. Browning had been right? If this was the site of a massacre?"

He put his hardhat on, then gave her a rueful look. "She told you that? About the aliens? Is that why you asked about the walls?"

"If there are alien ghosts, then you'll have some troubles when the End of the World opens."

"If there are alien ghosts, I'll get a lot of free publicity from the *Sci-Fi Channel* and the *Travel Channel*."

This time, she understood his tone. For all its lightness, it had some tension. He had thought about this. "It worried you, didn't it, when you dug this up?"

He nodded.

"Did you think she might be telling the truth?"

"Her version of it," he said. "Weren't you the one who told me that rumors hid real events? Maybe something bad had happened in Hope, and people made up the other story to cover it up."

"Not that anyone thought of aliens in 1908," Becca said.

He grinned, and slipped an arm around her. "Ever practical, aren't you, Becca?"

"Not ever," she said. Not during the drive from Mrs. Browning's to the coroner's office. Not when she remembered how that wall felt, squishy against her back.

"You never told me," she said. "Are you keeping the walls?"

"Why do you care?" he asked.

"They bother me," she said.

He looked at her. "You saw the alien ghosts."

She shook her head. "I didn't see anything. I just got scared as a teenager, is all."

He pulled her close. She didn't move away.

"Sometimes in old buildings," he said, "I feel like I can touch the past."

He wasn't looking at the ground any more. He was looking past the sunlight, into the desert itself.

"That's what you think that is?" Becca asked. "The past?"

"Or something," he said. "A bit of memory. A slice of time. Who knows? I always try to preserve that part of the old buildings, though."

"Why?" Becca asked.

"Because otherwise they're not worth saving. They're just wood or brick or marble. Ingredients. Buildings are living things, just like people."

She'd never heard mystical talk from him. Maybe she'd never listened.

"It's not about the money?" she asked.

"Becca, if it were about the money, I'd build cookie-cutter developments all over Hope and make millions." He shook his head. "It's about finding the surprises, whatever they might be. Good or bad."

"Or both," Becca said, moving some dirt at the edge of the hole.

"Or both," he said. "Sometimes I like both."

"Me too," she said. Then she studied him.

They were good together, but sometimes they were bad. She felt that longing for speed dial, then wondered if therapists were good and bad—good for some people, bad for others.

Maybe she should just trust herself.

She slid her hand into his.

He looked at her, surprised.

They stayed at the End of the World until the sun set—and waited for answers that might never ever come.

THEN

THE TRAIN HAD STOPPED in Hope for a long time before Jess Taylor found her. Her hand had molded to the railing near the door, and she couldn't remember how to set it free.

Besides, no one had unlocked the door for her. Apparently they thought it would be funny for her to climb over the edge to get off the train.

When he saw her, stuck there, her arm ending not in a hand but in a railing that went around the back of the train, he didn't say anything. Instead, he came up beside her. He hugged her, and she leaned into him.

He'd never hugged her before.

Then he set his own arm right next to hers, placing his hand right next to the place hers should be. And he watched as she shifted, slowly—fingers were so hard—and his body shielded hers from the platform, and all those other people meeting their families.

When she finished, and her arm fell at her side—complete with perfectly formed hand—he said, very softly, "They locked you out here, huh?"

She nodded and felt tears for the second time that day.

"I'm sorry. I didn't think they'd do that to a child."

And she thought of the End of the World, and all the children—the older children who had been her friends—and how they hadn't been locked out, they'd been *killed* and he'd helped bury them to keep his job, and she wondered how he could say something like that.

But she kept quiet. She was learning it was best to keep quiet sometimes.

"From now on," he was saying softly—she almost couldn't hear him over the engine, clanging as it cooled, "everyone'll think you're my niece from Mississippi. Try to talk like I do, and don't answer a lot of questions about back home. All right?"

"All right." She already knew this anyway. He'd told her before they went to Brothers.

"If we do this right," he said, pulling her close, "no one will ever know."

She swallowed, just like he did when he was nervous. No one would ever know. About her, about her family, about her people. No one would understand that for a while, her people waited and hoped.

Maybe she'd live to see the rescue ship come.

She wondered if she would recognize it.

She wondered if she would care.

Jess Taylor took her little bag with one hand, and with the other, he took her newly made hand.

"Chin up, Sarah," he said using the name she would hear from now on. In time, it would become her, just like the two arms and two legs and the permanent form and the dark skin would become her. Her self. Her identity.

She straightened her shoulders like he had taught her. She held her head high.

And then, clinging to Jess Taylor for support, she took her final steps away from the world she'd always known.

She took her first real steps into Hope.

ABOUT THE AUTHOR

INTERNATIONAL BESTSELLING WRITER Kristine Kathryn Rusch has won two Hugo awards, a World Fantasy Award, and six *Asimov's* Readers Choice Awards. Her latest science fiction novel is *Blowback*, the next novel in her Retrieval Artist series. She also writes mysteries under the name Kris Nelscott. For more information about her work, please go to kristinekathrynrusch.com.

Also by

Kristine Kathryn Rusch

Alien Influences
Snipers

The Retrieval Artist Series:

The Retrieval Artist (A Short Novel)
The Disappeared
Extremes
Consequences
Buried Deep
Paloma
Recovery Man
The Recovery Man's Bargain (A Short Novel)
Duplicate Effort
The Possession of Paavo Deshin (A Short Novel)
Anniversary Day
Blowback